MY BROTHER'S KEEPER (AMISH ROMANCE)

AMISH MISFITS BOOK #7

SAMANTHA PRICE

AMISH ROMANCE

CHAPTER 1

FROM HER WARM spot by the fire, Amy left off her sewing and glanced out the window at the gray sky. The cold wind was causing the trees by the barn to sway. The cooler October weather was finally here and Amy wasn't complaining. Besides huddling in front of the fireplace, she enjoyed going to bed early and listening to the wind tickling the shutters on the windows, the rain droplets dancing on the tin roof.

The only thing she didn't like was her nine-year-old brother's insistence on sitting on the porch no matter the weather. Once something was in Jonah's head that was it. Because of his fondness for sitting in that spot with the porch chair just so, she'd positioned her treadle sewing machine so she could better keep an eye on him. In the past, he'd wandered off on more than one occasion.

Amy often wondered if he sat there because he was

waiting for their parents to return. They never would, and she'd explained to him the best she could that they'd died. He was four at the time and most likely didn't understand it too much back then. But he knew now what death was and he was very logical-minded, so he couldn't be waiting for them, Amy decided.

A few seconds later, Amy knew what he was doing in that moment.

"Twenty-nine, thirty, thirty-one ..." His voice was barely audible when she didn't have her sewing machine operating.

Since he was staring out at the trees along the fence-line that separated the bishop's house from the Hershbergers' land, she guessed he was counting the fence posts. Although, it could've been the horizontal rows of wood planks that made up the walls of the barn. He was obsessed with numbers and was always counting something and loved arranging objects into patterns.

She pulled her mind off what Jonah was doing. Any minute, Lydia would be there to try on her wedding dress and she was expecting it to be finished except for the hem. The wedding was two weeks to the day from now, and Lydia's attempt at sewing her own dress had gone horribly wrong. Lydia had finally given up on the dress altogether after she'd managed to spill beet juice on it, which she later said was a blessing after Amy had agreed to take on the job of making the dress. When Amy's feet were operating the treadle it drowned out all other sound. She found the rhythm of the machine calming and when Jonah was at school, she became lost in her own world.

When Amy heard a voice, she stood up hoping it wasn't Lydia come early. Lydia wouldn't mind that she didn't have the dress up to the stage Amy had told her. It was Amy who would've been anxious. If her self-imposed deadlines weren't met, it caused her untold stress. Most people were like that, but along with the other compulsions she knew she had, this made Amy more understanding of her brother's world. Although she'd never disclosed her quirks to anyone, she guessed she had a touch of something not everyone had. Did she have something similar to her brother's condition? No one she knew had those compulsions, she was certain.

Amy would never tell anyone she had the obsessive need to pump the treadle three times before she threaded the needle and started sewing and then shake her hands three times when she stopped the machine. Forcing herself *not* to do those things wasn't worth the agony. At night, she turned lights off by turning them off, then on, and then off again. There was an urge— she had to do it that way, almost as though something bad would happen if she didn't.

She heaved a relieved sigh when she saw the visitor wasn't Lydia. It was just a man she didn't know. Living in the bishop's *grossdaddi haus,* she often had people from out of town come to her door looking for Bishop

Morgan. It didn't help matters that the bishop's house was built sideways and had two entrances, one at either end. And her entrance was the one closest to the barn.

She put her head down and started sewing once more. She didn't have a second to spare so she silently prayed the man wouldn't come to her door and disturb her concentration.

God had other plans. The man looked around and then headed to her house with a small suitcase in hand. Amy let out a groan at the irritation. All she had to do was finish off this one seam, then she'd answer the door and point the man to the bishop's doorway.

Knowing the man would talk to Jonah first she didn't intervene. She'd wait and see how Jonah coped with a stranger. The advice of his doctor was not to shield him too much from ordinary day-to-day events. Sometimes Jonah talked to people and sometimes he didn't. There was no telling what would happen.

"Is this Bishop Morgan's *haus?*" she heard the man ask Jonah above the hum of her machine.

Jonah gave no reply. He *would* choose this moment to keep silent.

"I'm coming," Amy called out. She glanced at the man through the window to see that he hadn't looked to see who'd called out and he was still looking at Jonah, undoubtedly waiting for a response.

The stranger took a step forward. "Did you hear what I said?" Out of the corner of her eye, she saw the man waving his hands in front of Jonah's face. "Are you stupid or something?" he snapped at Jonah.

Amy's blood boiled. She abruptly stopped sewing, rushed to the door and flung it open. She stomped toward him. "Why would you say that to him?"

The man took a step back taking off his hat to reveal a mop of sandy-colored curly hair. "Oh! I'm looking for the bishop."

"I kept calling out, 'I'm coming.' Didn't you hear that?"

"*Nee*. I didn't hear. I'm sorry." He looked down his straight nose at Jonah. "He won't answer me or even look at me. I simply asked if this is the bishop's *haus*."

"I don't care who you're looking for, and this is *not* the bishop's place. Why would you say something so horrible and mean to my *bruder*?"

The man focused his piercing blue-green eyes on her. "Your parents should instil some discipline into him. There's no greater shame for parents than disobedient *kinner*."

"My parents are with *Gott* and my *bruder* has autism."

His mouth dropped open. "I'm so sorry. I didn't mean to offend." He looked at Jonah, sympathetically this time. "I'm sorry. I don't know anything about autism. I have heard the name and that's about the sum of it."

She glared at him. There was still no excuse for

being so rude. "The bishop's entrance is at the opposite end of the *haus* from here. This is the *grossdaddi haus.*"

"Ah. It's hard to see that from the road." He pointed to the driveway. "The drive goes past your door first. That's why I thought this was the main entrance."

She folded her arms over her chest. Too angry to be gracious, she didn't tell him most people made that mistake. Besides his rudeness, he was wasting her time when she could've been sewing. "Well, it's not this entrance." She moved closer to her brother while still glaring at the stranger.

"Five," Jonah said staring into the distance.

"What did he say?" the man asked.

Amy shook her head. "It doesn't matter." The man had five buttons on his shirt and that's what Jonah had counted. Amy knew the man had come from far away because the Amish people in the surrounding vicinity used hook-and-eye fastenings or straight-pins on their clothes, never buttons.

"I'm just visiting Bishop Morgan and Fay, and I'll be staying for a few weeks. The last thing I want to do is get off on the wrong foot with people from around here."

That was her opportunity to ask where he'd come from but she was too irritated to stand there and talk politely, especially when she was behind on her work.

"I'm sorry for what I said. I've been traveling for what feels like days and I'm tired, downright grumpy, and, I'm sorry to say, that made me impatient." He stared at Amy waiting for a response.

Finally, when the man didn't move, she found her manners. "I'm Amy Lapp and this is my *bruder*, Jonah."

"I'm pleased to meet you and I'm very sorry for our upset. I'll find a way to make it up to you."

"I don't mean to be rude, but you can best 'make it up to me' by letting me get back to my work. I work from home and the last thing I need is interruptions."

A slight smile lifted the corners of his lips. "I'll remember that. It won't happen again, not by me." He slowly backed away.

"And you are?"

He laughed. "I'm sorry. Again. I'm Adam. I'm from—"

"I have work to get back to. I have a deadline." She glared at him and he backed away a little further.

"I won't bother you again." He gave a polite nod, turned and walked away.

She turned aside and as she reached the door, she looked back at him just as he glanced back over his shoulder. Their eyes met.

"It's Adam Brown," he called out, and then he turned and kept going.

"Just like *Dat*," Jonah said.

Shocked, Amy looked at Jonah and then looked back at the man as he rounded the corner of the house. He was tall, a man with a solid build just like their father'd had, and with the same light-colored curly hair. "Do you think so? I don't think he's anything like *Dat*." She looked at Jonah, and said softly, "I counted the five buttons too." Jonah looked into the distance and Amy wondered, as she often did, whether Jonah loved her or even knew she was his sister. Sometimes all she wanted was to hug him, but he hated that. "Now if you can sit still a little longer we'll go for that walk after Lydia comes. It'll be about three o'clock, okay?"

"Okay," Jonah said still looking at the trees.

To pre-empt any problems, she added, "I can't promise it will be right on the tic of three if I get held up." Amy hurried back inside, annoyed with the man and even more upset with herself that she'd let cold air into her house by leaving the door slightly open. She couldn't take the cold like her brother, who didn't seem to notice. After she'd sat down, she rubbed her hands to warm them before she took up where she'd left off.

CHAPTER 2

As Amy sewed, her mind wandered. It wasn't unusual for the bishop and Fay to have people staying at their house, but why was this man here? He had a suitcase, but it was pretty small. It didn't look like he was prepared to be here for a few weeks like he'd said. After pushing the stranger from her mind, she glanced through the window at Jonah. He said he'd wait until three, and he normally did what they agreed upon, but still, she couldn't risk him getting distracted and wandering off by himself again.

He'd stopped doing that since setting the standing agreement they'd go walking together every Saturday and Sunday, weather permitting.

It was two fifteen when Lydia pulled her buggy up outside the house.

This time it was convenient she was late because it had allowed Amy to get caught up to her personal goal on the dress. It was all done except the hem. Amy jumped up and slipped the dress onto the hanger, hung it on the hook she'd asked the bishop to put on the wall, and waited for Lydia to come inside. Lydia had been cheerful for the last three months, ever since she'd become engaged to Lionel Hershberger. They'd only been courting for a few months, and in secret. The wedding announcement had taken everybody by surprise, except for Lydia's close friends.

Lydia said hello to Jonah and then gave Amy a quick hug.

"Come in." Amy closed the door behind them and Lydia spied the dress and rushed to it.

"Is this it?" Lydia grabbed the dress and held the bottom of it out while it was still on the hanger.

"Of course that's it." Amy stepped forward and slipped the dress off the hanger and handed it to her.

"It's beautiful, truly beautiful." Lydia spun in a circle while holding it against herself.

"Good, I'm glad you like it. Try it on and we'll see how it fits. I haven't done the length yet. I wanted to see exactly how you wanted it."

"Not too long," Lydia said.

"Four inches below the knee?" That was the customary length in their community, although some women preferred their dresses longer, but never shorter.

"That's right." Lydia looked around. "Shall I try it on here?"

"*Jah*, it's only me here and Jonah won't move from the porch until we go for our walk later."

Lydia slipped the dress on over her head. It fit her well, not too tight and not too loose.

"How does it feel?" Amy asked.

Lydia swayed from side to side. "It's lovely and I like the feel of this material. What is it?"

"It's a special poly-cotton blend. It doesn't wrinkle so much."

"I like the sound of that."

"I thought you would. What do you think of the sleeve length?"

She put her hands down by her sides. "It's perfect."

"Good. I'll pin up the length, then. Can you stand on the stool?" After Lydia stepped up on the sturdy small stool, Amy sat on a second stool and used a long wooden ruler for her guide as she pinned up the hem. "There. Try that."

Lydia stepped down and swung from side to side again, and then walked around the room. "It's going to be perfect. It's a good length." She spun around to face Amy. "Does the color suit me?"

"*Jah*, it brings out your eyes."

Lydia giggled. "Good." Once she had changed back into her everyday dress, Lydia asked, "How are the *kapp* and apron coming along?"

Amy bit her lip. "I haven't started on them yet. I'll start on them tomorrow after I finish the hem."

"Is that leaving it a little late?"

"*Nee*. I'll get it finished. I don't have as much time as I'd like, but I can't make more hours in the day. Don't worry, they'll be done in time."

"*Denke*." Lydia handed the dress back to Amy and then Amy glanced at the clock. "Do you have time to stop and take a break?" Lydia asked.

"I can't today, sorry. I have to take Jonah for his walk at three and it's nearly that now. You know what he's like if he gets out of his routine."

"Okay. When shall I come back for the other things?"

"I would say … hmm. Today's Saturday, so I'd say they'll be finished Monday night—next Monday after this one coming." That would give her more than enough time.

Lydia clapped her hands together. "I'm so excited. I've got the best seamstress to sew my wedding dress. The attendants didn't mind sewing their own dresses, and *Mamm* said she'd help me with the men's suits, but I don't think we'll do a good job on them. We haven't even started."

"What?" Amy shrieked, guessing what would come next.

"You'll still have time to do them, won't you? I'm talking about the men's suits because the dresses are mostly finished."

Amy's breath caught in her throat. "What? This is the first time I've heard about this. Four suits? I can't. There simply isn't enough time." She held her hand to her heart, feeling like she couldn't breathe. "There's no time. No time at all."

"*Jah,* Amy. Don't you remember? We discussed it a few weeks ago."

They hadn't, because Amy would certainly have remembered. This was Lydia's way to cover up her error of organization. As much as she loved Lydia, she knew her friend had a way of bending the truth. "I don't think so. There was never any mention of the men's suits. I thought you'd found someone else to make them. Anyway, I don't normally do tailoring jobs."

"*Nee,* there is no one else."

Amy sighed, and then did another quick calculation. "There isn't time. Not to do it properly and I can't do a bad job, I just can't." Her stomach churned at the thought of late nights and early mornings making the suits. Even if she had no sleep and worked around the clock, she still wouldn't be able to meet the deadline. In her mind, she had an order of what she was doing for the next two weeks and none of it included suits. Men's suits were the hardest things to make.

"What if you only do Lionel's suit?"

Amy's breathing slowed. One suit was better than four, and she had nearly two weeks minus the Sundays and no other immediate jobs booked. She could do Lydia's cape, *kapp* and apron with her eyes closed. They wouldn't really take much time. "Okay, that would work even though it'll be rushed."

"You'll still do a good job, won't you?"

"I don't know any other way to sew. It will be just as good as all my other sewing. I'll need his measurements. If he's been properly fitted for a suit recently, he'll have his measurements. If not, he'll have to come here for me to do it, and as soon as he can." She shook her head, slightly annoyed with her friend.

"Denke, Amy, you're the best."

"I'll start it when I finish your other things, so get him, or the measurements to me by Monday, or Tuesday morning at the very latest. If you come a little earlier, we'll have time for a cup of coffee or something. You'll have to bring me the fabric then, too, and I can't sew the shirt. I won't have time."

"We might buy the shirt."

Amy nodded. "Good idea."

"How much fabric will you need for the suit?"

Amy said, "Three yards should be enough."

"Okay. I'll do that."

"Tell Mrs. Minter at the fabric store you'll need men's suit fabric. She'll show you a selection."

Lydia nodded. "Got it. I know the store you go to."

"How are all the other wedding plans coming along?" Amy felt a little bad she couldn't spend as much time with her friends as she wanted. They all lived carefree lives, but she sewed every spare moment to make a living. It was good of the bishop to give her and Jonah the place to live, but she couldn't stay here forever. Although when the time came to move, she knew it would take ages for Jonah to get used to it because he wasn't good with changes.

Jonah liked living where they were. He liked wandering around the bishop's paddocks and the ones on the neighboring Hershberger property where Lionel, Lydia's fiancé, lived with his parents.

"*Mamm's* organizing the food along with Aunt Millie. You really should get out more, so you can meet someone too. You won't find a husband surrounded by these four walls. It's not as though someone is going to come knocking on your door."

"I really can't. I go out on Sundays and then take Jonah to his medical appointments once a month on the first Thursday. Then I take him to Tabitha for his natural herbal remedies, and otherwise I work. There's little time for anything else."

Lydia sighed. "How are you ever going to find a man?"

Amy shook her head and smiled at the concern on her friend's face. "It'll happen when and if it happens; according to *Gott's* plan." It was the last thing she needed to think about. It was something everyone else seemed worried about on her behalf, and she was pleased to let them do so.

"Never mind, you might meet someone at my wedding. I've got lots of cousins coming from Ohio."

Amy nodded and kept her concerns to herself. Even though most Amish girls married as early as they could, it wasn't practical for her, not with Jonah to care for.

There was no other caretaker for Jonah and unless she found a man who could fit in with their sometimes-chaotic life, it wouldn't work. And moving to another community, even for undying love and the best man in the world, was simply out of the question. Jonah would never adapt to a place he didn't know. It would be too traumatic for him to try.

Amy glanced at the clock. "It's three. I'll have to go for that walk." Amy grabbed her black shawl, and when Lydia and Amy reached the front door, Jonah was standing there waiting for her and moving from foot to foot impatiently, ready to go.

Amy hugged Lydia goodbye and waited until she drove away.

CHAPTER 3

Amy looked over at Jonah, who had already started walking. "Ready?"

"*Jah.*"

"Let's go." She followed Jonah while wrapping herself in her shawl to keep out the cold. When they were a distance from the house, Amy said, "We've forgotten the sack."

Jonah stopped and looked around.

"Don't worry, I'll help you carry anything you find."

Jonah turned back around and kept walking. They normally carried an empty grain sack so Jonah could carry all his findings back with him. His favorites were the smooth rounded pebbles that were closer to the small river that ran down the back of the property.

Amy kept a distance from Jonah because on their walks he preferred to walk in front, and alone. Although, she mused, he walked with the bishop's boys to school and didn't need to be in front of them. He walked with them side-by-side.

Once they got to the other side of the barn, they slipped through the wire fence that separated the neighboring farm from the bishop's land. The Hershbergers had cows in their paddock and the animals always stared as Jonah and Amy walked through their domain. Sometimes the cows stepped a couple of paces toward them but never got closer than that.

Their walk normally took an hour. During that hour, Amy would talk to Jonah about her day and never expect a response. She rarely got one. Today, she grumbled about having to sew Lionel's suit at such short notice.

She pulled her shawl tighter around herself, looking forward to the snow. It was the only time Jonah wouldn't go for his walks. Instead, he'd sit on the porch, or if it was too cold for that, he'd sit by one of the windows looking out.

Amy stared at Jonah methodically placing one foot after the other, and she wondered what it was like inside his mind. He didn't show emotions except to be upset when things didn't go as planned. She had memories of him laughing on very rare occasions before their parents died, but never since.

There were never any two-way conversations between them. He would answer her questions but he rarely started off a conversation. Most of his talk was yes or no, or asking for something he wanted in as few words as possible. That made Amy feel alone and she was grateful to have her close friends. The bishop and his wife had become like her parents. They were always watching over her and lending their support wherever they could.

Jonah leaned down to pick up a pebble, and Amy said, "Can I see that, Jonah?" He turned and showed it to her briefly before he closed his fingers around it. "That was a pretty one, wasn't it?"

He didn't answer, turned away and continued walking.

She asked him, "What do you think about Adam, hmm?" There was no answer. It was like talking to herself. He'd heard her and she wondered what Jonah thought of her talking to him about a man—a possible husband. "He seemed nice enough I suppose, and he did apologize for being weird. I can understand his behavior if he was frustrated, tired and cranky. We all get like that now and again when things try us, but what is he doing here in Lancaster County I wonder? He's here by himself with no family members and staying with the bishop."

"He's been bad," Jonah said.

Amy was amused at his words. "You think he's been bad, and his parents have sent him to the bishop for him to correct his behavior?"

"*Jah.*"

Amy stifled a giggle. It was a rare moment he commented on things, so she figured Adam must've

19

touched something inside him. "Why bad? Don't you like him? He seems nice enough." Jonah didn't answer. Instead, he walked on, and on, and on, without saying another word. He collected around fifteen pebbles and Amy ended up with them tucked into her shawl. "How far are we going today? I think it's time we turned back."

"A little further," Jonah said.

"Okay, but just a little way."

Since Jonah had made the effort to speak, she'd do what he asked.

THAT AFTERNOON they'd been home for an hour when Amy looked out the window and saw the annoying stranger walking up to her front door. Jonah was now sitting on the rug between the fireplace and the couch looking at the collection of pebbles he'd brought home.

Amy left Lydia's wedding dress on the table where she'd been hemming it and hurried to the door. When she opened it, Adam was just about to knock. "Hello, Adam."

"I called around earlier, but you weren't home."

She hoped he wasn't going to make 'calling around' a habit while he was staying with the bishop. "We were on our walk."

Adam glanced inside at Jonah who was now

arranging his new supply of pebbles into rows across the rug. "What's he doing?"

"He collects small stones and makes patterns with them. That's one of his favorite things to do."

"I see. And what else does Jonah like to do? I know nothing about autism." He rubbed his jaw.

She turned around and glanced at Jonah, then remembered what his doctor said, and looked back at Adam. "You can ask him if you want."

He raised his eyebrows. "Can I?"

"Of course."

Adam leaned forward, and whispered to Amy, "Can he understand what I'm saying?"

"He understands everything. He's very intelligent. It's just that he has trouble expressing himself and doesn't know what to do in certain situations. He might answer you but don't be too worried if he doesn't. Sometimes it takes him a long time to answer." She tapped her head, and whispered, "He's thinking what to say."

"Interesting. I'd like to learn more."

"Why?" The question slipped out and she hoped he didn't think she was rude. No one else except her close friends had been interested in Jonah. People normally left them alone. He shrugged his shoulders and then looked downward and Amy felt bad for embarrassing him. "I'm sorry, that was probably rude. Sometimes I don't think before I speak. I really should stop and listen to the words in my head before I allow myself to say them, but if I did that I might not say anything at all."

He gave a little chuckle. "I think we've all been guilty of speaking without thinking at times. Would you mind if I come in to speak with Jonah?"

"That would be okay." She opened the door wide enough to allow him through.

He crouched down near Jonah. "It's me again, Jonah. It's Adam." Jonah didn't answer or look up at him, and Adam glanced up at Amy, who was leaning against the wall listening. After an encouraging nod from Amy, he looked back at Jonah. "Have you ever climbed a tree?"

He kept arranging his rocks. *"Nee."*

Adam lowered himself to a seated position next to Jonah with his legs out straight. "That's something I loved to do when I was about your age. My brothers and I climbed trees. There was one tree in particular that was our favorite. It had low spreading branches and it was easy to get up onto the first branch and then the next branch and then the next. Soon we were at the very top of the tree."

Amy thought she'd help Adam out. Jonah might join in the conversation once it was started. "Was it scary?" Amy asked moving to the couch.

"It was, the first few times until we got used to it. Actually, it probably wasn't a very good idea. It mightn't have been very safe if we fell from the top. We never fell though. That's what we did for fun and then we'd also kick a ball around. In winter, we'd ice skate and slide on the snow on boards we'd made." He stopped speaking for a moment. "Have you ever done anything like that, Jonah?"

"Nee."

"If you tried things like that, you might find you like them. What if I take you and your friends out one time and find some fun things to do?"

Jonah didn't answer, and Amy was a little annoyed that Adam hadn't asked her first if he could take Jonah out. She didn't like the thought of him going off somewhere with a stranger and even though the bishop knew Adam, he was still a stranger to her. It might have been okay if Jonah was more like other boys his age. At least the man was showing an interest, but he needed to understand and experience what Jonah was like before he offered to do things with him.

At first, she was worried Adam was giving Jonah ideas about climbing trees and other ideas that would only make him feel more different if he didn't attempt them or didn't like them. Still, Amy couldn't be too angry with Adam since the bishop and his sons were the only other males who'd made an effort to get to know him. It was different with the bishop's sons because they'd grown up with Jonah. Since Jonah often didn't speak to people, it was a good sign he had spoken to Adam.

"Would you like a hot chocolate, Adam? I'm just about to make Jonah one."

"Nee denke. I should go."

"Okay. It was nice of you to stop by."

"Bye, Jonah."

"Bye," Jonah said.

Adam flashed Amy a smile, stood and straightened his trousers. "I might see you tomorrow."

She nodded not wanting to encourage these unannounced visits, and then showed him out. When he was a few yards from the house, she hurried over to him. "Wait, Adam." He turned around. "Jonah is uncoordinated and can't climb or kick a ball. He's not interested in those things like other boys are. He likes science and numbers. The teacher says he's interested in that kind of thing and he loves patterns."

"I can see that from what he was doing with the rocks. I appreciate you telling me." He stared at her. "Would you rather I didn't try to interact with him?"

"Nee. I do want you to. I'm pleased you are. I'm just protective and worried about him and how he's going to react to different things, and well … and different people."

"I think he and I are getting along nicely."

She smiled at him. "You have gotten a good reaction out of him so far. He spoke to you, and he seldom speaks to new people."

"That's good." He pointed at her. "And it's nice to see a smile on your face. You're a lot less scary when you smile."

A giggle escaped her lips. "When Jonah's doing okay, I'm happy."

"If I can help, I will."

"Denke, Adam." She turned and walked back to the house. When she walked inside, Jonah was nowhere to be seen and his pile of rocks was abandoned on the rug. Noises drew her to the kitchen and she found him there attempting to make his own hot chocolate. After taking a deep breath, she stepped forward and guided him on making it rather than taking over the task.

LATE THAT SATURDAY night after Jonah had gone to bed, there was a gentle knock on Amy's front door. She opened it to see the bishop's wife, Fay.

"I'm sorry for the late hour, but would you take Liza to the meeting in the morning? I've only just realized we have one more person than the buggy can take."

"Ah, of course, you have the extra visitor." Liza was the oldest daughter. Jonah always traveled with the bishop's family and flat out refused to go to a meeting unless he went with them. "You will take Jonah, though?"

"Of course, same as always. I always include him in the passenger count with my boys."

"Okay. I'll wait for her in the buggy in the morning." Fay smiled at her. *"Denke,* Amy."

"Anytime. I'm happy to help whenever I can."

Fay gave her another big smile and hurried back

down the porch steps. Amy closed the door and looked back at the sewing. "Another half an hour should do it," she said aloud. She picked up her small alarm clock and put the timer on for thirty minutes, then sat down and continued sewing the hem. Amy had learned to go to bed early if she wanted to get any sleep at all because Jonah had a habit of waking during the night. He never left his room, but the clicking noises as he arranged his stones or other items into patterns would disturb her and prevent her from falling asleep. If she was already asleep, she wouldn't wake.

CHAPTER 4

AFTER THEIR NORMAL Sunday morning routine of getting ready for the meeting, Jonah headed to the bishop's buggy. He crossed paths with Liza, who was hurrying in the opposite direction toward Amy's buggy. Jonah always made his way over to the bishop's house early in the morning on meeting Sundays, after he had eaten his breakfast, and then he sat on their porch until they all got in the buggy. Jonah had gotten into the routine of traveling in their buggy to Sunday meetings before Amy had bought a good used buggy of their own. The first Sunday they were living there, a friend had stopped by to take them to the meeting. Amy went with the friend, but Jonah wanted to travel with the bishop's boys, most likely because he knew them from school. From then on, Jonah traveled in the bishop's buggy and that had become his ingrained habit.

"*Denke* for taking me," twelve-year-old Liza said as she climbed into Amy's waiting buggy.

"It's a pleasure. And you've got a visitor staying at your *haus?*" She moved the buggy away from the barn and waited for all the people to get into the bishop's buggy.

"*Jah*, his name is … I forget."

Amy giggled. "You forget?"

"Adam, that's right. I'll have to remember his name by remembering Adam and Eve."

"That's a good way to remember the name. And why's he visiting?"

"That, I haven't been able to find out yet."

Amy giggled again. "You must have your suspicions."

"I'm not allowed to pry and I can't even eavesdrop, so it gets a little difficult sometimes." Liza lowered her voice. "He might have done something bad and his parents sent him to *Dat* for him to get straightened out."

"Oh, that's what Jonah said when I asked him, but I think Adam's a little too old for that. Does he seem like the kind of man who might've done something bad?" Amy looked over at Jonah, who'd just climbed into the other buggy. She always felt better keeping an eye on him even though she knew he'd be safe traveling with the bishop's family.

Liza screwed up her face. "I suppose not. He could

be here looking for a new place to live; maybe he's been run out of his own community."

Amy couldn't keep the smile from her face. "That sounds similar to the first reason you had."

"We might find out more today if *Dat* makes an announcement about him."

"We?"

Liza nodded.

"I'm not the slightest bit interested in why he's here." Amy scoffed and glanced again at her brother who was now in the back of the buggy and looking out. She was glad Jonah had gotten into the buggy with Adam there, since Adam was still little more than a stranger to him. That was a huge step forward. Last time the bishop had a visitor traveling in the buggy with them, Jonah had refused to get in and she and Jonah had to miss the meeting altogether.

"Aren't you at least a little bit curious?" Liza asked.

Amy shook her head, and then followed the bishop's buggy onto the road. *"Nee."*

"Even just a tiny little bit interested? I'm not saying you're interested in him as a man, just curious to know why he's here. You've got to be."

"Maybe just a teeny tiny little bit, but that's all."

When they arrived at the Jones's house where the meeting was being hosted, Amy parked her buggy at the end of one of the many rows of buggies. Liza immediately thanked her and headed off to find her friends, and then Amy watched as Jonah walked with the bishop's son, Elroy, into the house. Jonah always sat in the third row from the front next to Elroy, who was the same age.

Amy sat with her usual friends while keeping an eye on Jonah. When the meeting was over, Amy watched Adam to see who he'd talk with. She was still intrigued to know why he was there despite denying it to Liza. The bishop had announced that Adam was visiting from Oakland County for a few weeks and that was all he said. No reason for his stay was given.

Amy noticed Adam seemed quite friendly with Sarah Yoder's parents. Sarah was due to arrive back any day from her vacation with her aunt in Walnut Creek, Ohio. After Adam walked away, Amy wandered over to Sarah's mother, Tabitha.

"Hello. How's Sarah?"

Tabitha gritted her teeth. "Oh, that girl! She called home yesterday and said she's delaying coming home for another week." She shook her head and drew her lips tightly together showing she was opposed to the idea.

"She's been there awhile now."

"She's been there for four months and it's high time she came home."

Amy nodded. "Do you know Adam? I saw you talking with him just now."

Tabitha's frown was replaced with a grin. "I grew up with Adam's *mudder* and we have remained close friends."

"Oh, I didn't know. You must know Adam quite well, then?"

"*Jah*. We've met quite a few times and so has Sarah." Tabitha narrowed her eyes at her. "Why do you ask?"

"No particular reason. I was just curious as to why he's here."

Tabitha looked over Amy's shoulder. "Jonah's walking away."

Amy's heart nearly stopped. "*Ach! Denke,* and excuse me." She walked as fast as she could to catch up with Jonah, upset with herself for being so distracted about Adam that she had forgotten to keep an eye on him. She'd lost him once when he was four and that was the worst feeling in the world. It was a few months after their parents had died, and the bishop had found Jonah wandering and brought him home. Amy, only fifteen herself at that time, had felt deeply guilty and embarrassed. When the bishop saw how they were living he insisted they come back and live in his *grossdaddi haus*—a self-contained two-bedroom living space built onto the side of his house.

When Amy caught up with Jonah, she grabbed him by the shoulder. He whimpered, ducking away from her. He didn't like anybody touching him, not even his sister, but sometimes it was unavoidable. The doctor told her it had something to do with hypersensitive or "overloaded" nerves, and that a touch that would feel normal to someone without autism felt too intense to

Jonah. "You can't wander away like that, Jonah. I told you before." Jonah turned around. "Now, follow me." Amy started walking back to the Jones's house. Then she glanced over her shoulder and was relieved he was following her. "We can walk at three o'clock today when we get home, but you can't go walking off by yourself." He was looking off to the side instead of at her, but she knew he'd heard.

CHAPTER 5

WHEN THEY GOT BACK to the crowd, Adam approached her. "There you are; I was looking for you."

As she stood talking to him, Jonah charged past. Amy looked over and saw the food being placed on the trestle tables. Jonah had a healthy appetite and she knew he wouldn't go away now the food was there. She could relax for a few minutes. "You were looking for me?" she asked Adam, still careful to keep one eye on Jonah.

"*Jah.*"

"Do you want to say you're sorry again?" She smiled at him, but inside she was still feeling stirred up with anxiety over Jonah wandering off.

Adam chuckled. "I do. I still feel dreadful. I want to explain. I was only like that because I was tired and cranky. I'd been traveling for hours and I'd already gone

33

SAMANTHA PRICE

to about three wrong places and when Jonah wouldn't answer me I just thought he was a disobedient child."

"I know, I heard what you said to him."

His gaze dropped to the ground and he shook his head. "I feel like a beast for it. I'm usually a very patient man. Fay told me a bit about you and your family."

She glanced over at Fay who was helping lay out the food, then looked back at Adam. "There's not much to tell really. My parents died four … *nee,* it must be five years ago now, and since then it's just been Jonah and me. That's as exciting as it gets. What about you?" She didn't like talking about herself.

"Fay said they died within days of each other from pneumonia."

Amy nodded. "They did. It was like an epidemic that year. Many people in the community had it. It spread like a fire. It was only my parents who died from it, sadly. Oh!" Amy's hands flew to her face. "I don't mean I think more people should've died. I just would've preferred it if mine hadn't."

"I know what you mean, don't worry. My parents are still very much alive and I have four brothers and four sisters. I am the one in the middle."

"And does that have something to do with you normally being patient?"

He laughed. "Possibly. I really would like to make it up to you in some way."

"*Nee.* Forget about it. It's truly not necessary. If

34

people have never met anyone like Jonah it's only natural for them not to know."

"*Jah*, but there was no reason for me to be rude."

"That's right. There wasn't. Except, you gave a reason." She noticed how upset he was and was sorry for him. He did seem a decent kind of man. "Let's just forget about it, shall we? I've accepted your apology. We can't keep going back and forward talking about this." She didn't know how Adam could undo what he'd already said to Jonah. If only people were more aware of others, but they weren't, and Jonah couldn't live in a bubble. "His doctor said he has to live with people and mix with people, so of course he will come across people who don't understand him and people who are rude and possibly worse. I can't shield him too much."

"But I don't want to be one of those people. I'd like to get to know him better, but it seems it's not going to be easy."

"He's in his own little world. Sometimes I just want to keep him safe at home away from everyone and everything, but I can't."

Adam looked over at Jonah. "He seems to be doing okay."

"He's okay when he's in a familiar place with people he knows."

He looked back at her. "It can't be easy for you raising him with your parents not around to help."

"We manage."

"You're doing a good job."

She smiled. *"Denke."* It meant a lot to hear those words. It was so hard constantly being on guard and watching over him, and she'd been young herself when she'd become Jonah's sole caregiver. That's why it was such a blessing for her to be able to breathe easy when he was at school. The teacher didn't insist that he join in with anything and was understanding, and even took time to explain whatever Jonah asked. There was an awkward silence and Amy didn't know what to say to fill it.

Adam rubbed his forehead. "I should get some food I suppose."

"Jah, you should before Jonah eats it all."

They shared a little chuckle and then they parted. Jonah had taken his full plate and sat down at one of the nearby tables and Amy made her way over and sat down with him. "Ah, that looks good."

He didn't say anything and kept eating. Amy didn't get food for herself until after Adam had sat down. She took particular interest where he sat and noticed he sat with Sarah's parents.

As Amy filled her plate with a slice of pizza pie and a little salad, she put pieces of information together like a giant puzzle. Sarah's mother, Tabitha, had looked a little upset when Amy asked questions about Adam, and Tabitha and Adam's mother were close. Could Sarah's mother be hoping Sarah would get back from Walnut Creek in a hurry, so she could see Adam before he left? Tabitha had acted very upset that Sarah had delayed coming home.

A few minutes later, Liza slumped down at the table next to her.

"What's the matter with you?" Amy asked.

"Mrs. Greuller's chocolate cake."

"What about it?"

Liza's mouth turned down at the corners. "It's all gone."

"Oh." Amy had to work hard to keep from laughing at her young friend's woeful face.

"You should've seen it, Amy. It was a chocolate mousse cake with little marshmallows dotted around the top. She only brought one. Last time she made one I missed out on it, too."

"Surely there's a piece left." She looked at Jonah's empty plate. "Get more if you want, Jonah."

Jonah didn't need to be asked twice. He bounded to his feet and walked over to get more food.

Liza continued, *"Nee.* I was waiting in a queue for the bathroom and by the time I got back to the dessert table it had all gone. It's the best chocolate cake in the world and she only made one."

Right at that moment, a plate of chocolate cake that met Liza's description was placed on the table and Amy looked up and saw Adam. He then sat down next to Liza.

"Where did that come from?" Liza's eyes were glued to the cake.

"Someone put a piece aside for me telling me I just had to eat a piece of this most amazing cake Mrs. Greuller made."

"Can I have some please? Just a little taste?" Liza whined. "I went to get some of that, but it was all gone."

He chuckled and pushed the plate toward her. "It's for you."

Her eyebrows flew up. "For me?"

He stopped pushing it. "There *is* one little condition. I do have a favor to ask."

"Anything. You just name it. What is it?"

"You go home in your parents' buggy and I go home with Amy. We'll swap buggy places."

CHAPTER 6

Liza stared at Adam. "Is that all? If I agree to that you'll give me the cake? The whole piece?"

"*Jah.*"

"Is that all right, Amy? Please say yes. Please, please, please?"

Amy giggled. "It must be quite some cake. It's all right with me if your folks don't mind."

"It'll be okay with them. They won't care a bit." Liza reached out and pulled the plate to herself.

Amy watched as Liza pushed the cake fork into the cake, carefully adding some of the frosting and collected the cream in the middle. Then she opened her mouth, pushed it in, closed her lips and slid the fork free. As she lowered her fork to the plate, she closed her eyes savoring the taste.

Amy looked at Adam, who was also watching Liza, and she saw his lips rising at the corners. Then he caught her eye and they shared a moment. It seemed Adam was doing everything he could to gain her attention and now he had it. No one had ever been like that with her and she liked it.

In the meantime, Jonah had sat down with a small helping of peas and nothing else.

Adam looked over at Amy. "I suppose I should ask you. May I travel home with you, Amy?"

"Amy won't mind," Liza said having just swallowed her mouthful.

Amy laughed. "I'll take you back to the bishop's *haus*, Adam Brown."

With amusement, Adam told Liza, "You see, Liza, I've made Amy cranky with me before and I think she's still upset with me. That's why I have to be extra careful."

Liza wasn't listening. All she could think about was the cake. "You two should try this cake. I've never had anything like it. Everyone was right about it. I wonder if she'll give me the recipe."

Amy giggled. "I'm not upset, Adam, and Liza doesn't care anything about what you just said."

With another mouthful, Liza covered her lips politely with her fingertips, and managed to say, "Don't be angry with him, Amy. This is so delicious! Do you want to try some?"

Amy looked down at the rich, dark dessert. "I wouldn't want to deprive you of any. You're enjoying it way too much. What if I had a taste and then couldn't stop there?"

Liza giggled at Amy's teasing. "Adam? Do you want a piece?"

He chuckled and shook his head. *"Nee denke."*

"Would you like a taste of this cake, Jonah?" Liza asked pushing the plate toward him.

Amy was touched by Liza's unfeigned kindness in asking Jonah, too.

"Nee." Jonah said after a while. He was more preoccupied with trying to get peas onto his fork.

"Looks like I have this large piece all to myself. *Denke,* Adam. You can come stay with my *familye* anytime."

Adam chuckled once more. *"Gut!* I'm enjoying my stay here in Lancaster County. I'll have to tell Mrs. Greuller she has to make more than one cake next time."

"Oh, and you're going to tell her that, are you? You can't have met her yet," Liza said. "That's her over there in the dark blue dress."

Adam followed Liza's stretched out hand to Mrs. Greuller, a short stout lady who wore a grim expression. "Maybe I won't tell her, but perhaps someone should."

"It's not gonna be me," said Amy.

"Nee," Adam said. "Mrs. Greuller looks as though she wouldn't be used to anyone suggesting that she do anything."

"I'm sure she's okay when you talk with her," Amy said.

Liza finished the last of her cake, scraping up every last trace. "That was delicious." She stood up, and said, "I'll just let *Mamm* know you're driving Adam home, Amy."

"Okay, *denke*. I would appreciate that."

"*Denke* for the cake, Adam, once again. I'll make you seconds for desserts for the entire week."

Adam laughed. "Okay. I'd like that."

Liza left the three of them alone. Jonah was still chasing peas around his plate with his fork.

"That was very smooth how you arranged all that." Amy smiled at Adam.

"I know. I hope you don't mind, but I want to spend more time with you."

"I don't mind at all."

"I was pleased with myself." Adam chuckled. "Who knew chocolate cake could open so many doors? It's a good thing I didn't taste it first or I might have been unable to give it to Liza." He looked over at Jonah. "Do you like cake, Jonah?"

Jonah shook his head.

"Sometimes he does," Amy said. "But we're trying to eat healthier these days and not have so many sugary things. Tabitha's got him on a special diet. It's not a restrictive diet. Well, not too restrictive. We're just cutting down on certain foods. We go to Tabitha for his health. She gives him herbs and special herbal tonics.

We're trying all we can to be extra healthy, aren't we, Jonah?"

"*Jah.*"

Adam said, "I believe it's all about moderation. Surely some sweets now and again won't hurt?"

Amy shrugged. "I guess." She wasn't going to start telling Adam, in front of Jonah, all of the supplements he was on and why. Adam clearly wasn't in agreement with such things. Amy believed strongly that *Gott's* plants were medicinal and people like Tabitha had a special gift for using them for good health. Anything that might do Jonah good was worth trying and that included eating the right foods.

"Are you staying on for the singing, Amy?"

"Oh, you didn't think I was staying, did you? Is that why you arranged to go home with me?"

"*Nee*, I just thought about it now. I didn't want to stay, but I will if you do."

She shook her head. "I've got to get home early. Jonah and I have our routine, you know?"

"*Jah.*" Adam nodded. "Routine is very important for *kinner.*"

"Especially for Jonah because he likes things all the same, and at the same time. Don't you, Jonah?"

"*Jah.*"

When she saw Jonah stab the last pea, Amy said, "You can take your plate back over now." Jonah stood and headed back to the food table. "And what do you think of our community so far?" Amy asked Adam.

"That's something I've been asked about twenty times today."

Amy laughed. "Ah, I'm sorry. I didn't mean to be so unoriginal."

"*Nee*, don't be sorry. You asked in a much sweeter voice than everybody else. I have been here before as I think I might've told you. I like it a lot." He looked around. "There are a few people I should say hello to before it's time to go."

"Okay. I'll be waiting right here for you."

He gave her a smile and left the table just as Jonah sat back down with a small piece of cake. It wasn't anything like Mrs. Grueller's chocolate cake. It was a mini cupcake with a tiny layer of frosting. He must've listened to what Adam said because he normally didn't eat such things.

"Well, what do think about that, Jonah? Adam's going home with me in my buggy because he's swapping places with Liza."

Jonah didn't say a word.

Bishop Morgan was always the last to leave a meeting because so many people wanted to speak with him. Amy couldn't leave until the bishop did because she liked to follow their buggy since Jonah would be in it. That way, she arrived home at the same time as Jonah.

When the bishop's children ran to their buggy, Adam walked over to Amy. "Are we ready?" he asked.

"We are. Well, I am." She stood up, looking at Jonah

who was now getting into the buggy with the bishop's children.

Adam said, "Ah, it'll be just the two of us in the buggy and that's just how I like things."

She smiled weakly and hoped he didn't mean that he didn't like Jonah around. He seemed to like her and he would be a stupid man if he didn't realize that she and Jonah came as a package. Jonah would always come first in her life. Her whole life centered around Jonah and it could never be any other way.

As they approached her horse and buggy, he said, "Let me drive?"

She stared at him shocked. "Why?"

"I'm a man and the man should drive the buggy."

She laughed at him. "It's my buggy, so I'll drive it."

"I'm not joking."

"You really think the man should drive? It's not a date or anything. I'm just driving you home because you bribed our young friend with chocolate cake." She grimaced when she heard that come out of her mouth. If he was offended, things between them would be ruined before they even began. Part of her wanted something to begin between them if that was at all a possibility. Would she ever learn to keep her mouth closed?

"Okay. I agree. It's not a date. Very true. And we should do that sometime. We should go on a date. That was a good idea of yours."

She got up into the buggy not knowing what to say.

He didn't name a time for a date and he didn't ask her what she thought about going on one. And he said it as though the whole thing had been her idea.

Once she'd taken hold of the reins, he said, "No need to say anything. I know you didn't really have a choice in taking me home and I forced this alone time with you."

"I'm glad to get to know you a little better." She figured he'd put himself out, so she needed to give him some encouragement rather than being so hard on him all the time.

He turned his body slightly to face her. "I'm pleased you're not too upset with me."

"I'm not. It's okay."

They traveled through the tree-lined streets with the bishop's buggy a little ways ahead. Amy found herself wanting the drive to be longer than it was, so she could spend more time with him. It would've been nice if they had a few hours to spend together rather than the several minutes it took from the Jones's house to hers.

When they got home, Adam asked, "Since you wouldn't let me drive can I at least unhitch the buggy for you?"

That was one of her least favorite chores. "All right. If you feel the need to do that … as a man."

He chuckled. "I kind of do."

"You're very welcome to do that and rub down the

horse. If that's what you'd like to do." She jumped down from the buggy.

"I would feel useful," she heard him say from within the buggy.

"Good. Consider yourself useful."

He chuckled and stepped down. After she told him what paddock the horse went into and where the buggy went, she headed to her place with Jonah, who'd been waiting for her near the barn.

CHAPTER 7

THAT AFTERNOON, when Amy and Jonah were setting off on their three o'clock walk, Adam yelled out to them to wait. Amy stopped in her tracks while Jonah kept walking, ignoring him completely.

When Adam caught up with her, he asked, "Where are you going?"

"Just for another walk. We walk at the same time every day." She started walking behind Jonah and Adam walked along beside her.

"Where are you headed?"

"Just wherever Jonah wants."

Adam pulled a quizzical face.

"What have you been doing this afternoon?" she asked, hoping to get a hint of why he was visiting. It seemed that no one knew.

"I haven't done anything since the meeting. And yourself?"

"Just went to the meeting and that's all. I can't sew on a Sunday, because it's work, but tomorrow I'll be right back onto sewing Lionel's suit for the wedding. Lydia just sprang it on me. It was all last minute." She knew she looked unhappy, and tried not to get stressed about all the work ahead of her. "I guess you'll still be here for their wedding on Saturday?"

"*Jah.* You must be very good at sewing."

"I am." When he looked at her surprised, she added, "I guess I am because people keep coming back and they recommend me. I'm not prideful."

"*Ach nee.* It's rare to find a woman who speaks so honestly about herself. I didn't think you were being prideful."

"Good."

"How did you and Jonah end up living at the bishop's *haus?*"

"If I answer that you'll have to tell me why you're here visiting the bishop."

He adjusted the collar of his shirt, pulling at it as though it was strangling him. And then he gave a funny smile. She knew he didn't want to tell her and there could only be one reason. He was looking for a wife. As much as she was growing fond of him, she had to tell him it wasn't going to be her. It was tempting to talk with him and have those butterflies in her tummy, but it wasn't practical to set both of them up for a failed relationship. If that's why he was talking with her, and seeking her out, he was wasting his time.

Before he spoke again, she said, "What my *bruder* has is genetic. If I had *kinner,* it could be passed on."

He stared at Jonah. "He doesn't look like he's suffering anything too badly."

"He does suffer. It's not easy for him to fit in. And people treat him as though he's stupid and he's not. Things are difficult for him sometimes. He has anxiety and has panic attacks when things get too much for him."

"What kinds of things?"

She shrugged her shoulders. "To you and me it would be nothing, but to Jonah those things are huge. It's whenever things don't go how he wants them. Usually when things are different from how he thinks they're going to be. Like, for instance, traveling with the bishop to a Sunday meeting. He won't go with me, his own *schweschder.*"

"Jonah is the first person I've met like this."

She saw on Adam's face he was again feeling bad about yesterday. "You're not the first person who was rude to him and unfortunately you won't be the last. It was a genuine mistake and no one is holding anything against you." She hoped she'd made him feel better and also turned him off the idea of liking her, if he'd been thinking that way. He was definitely showing signs of being attracted to her and there was no other reason she could think of that he'd be spending so much time with her. If he wasn't there looking for a wife, the only other thing was looking for work, but he hadn't mentioned that. "What kind of work do you do?"

"I make buggies."

"I've never met a buggy maker before. I bought mine used. Do you build them from start to finish?"

He shook his head. "No one does that anymore. Not that I'm aware of. Different components are made in different places and someone like me puts them together. Don't get me wrong, it's still a lot of work and there's a lot of skill involved."

"I'm sure there is. It sounds interesting and a little creative, kind of like what I do."

"It's really not interesting or creative." Adam laughed. "It's all just the same routine every day."

"Oh. Well, at least it's a job."

"That's true. And I can't complain. I like meeting the people who come to buy the buggies. I do meet some interesting people and it provides me with a good income."

Adam walked the whole way with them and then back to the house. She enjoyed her time with him, but she still hadn't found out what he was doing there. He had a job and that's all she'd found out. He didn't mention a girlfriend, and from the way he was asking her about her life, she doubted he had one.

CHAPTER 8

AMY WAS JUST FINISHING off the ties on Lydia's wedding prayer *kapp* on Monday evening when there was a knock on her door. "Good timing," she said to herself as she took up her scissors and snipped off the final thread. Then she hurried to the door and saw Lydia standing there. As Lydia walked through the doorway, Amy noticed she had a bundle wrapped in brown paper under her arm. "That's the suit fabric I hope."

"Hello, to you."

Amy laughed. "Hello, Lydia. Sorry, I've got my mind on the job. You've got the material?"

Lydia stared at her and raised her dark eyebrows. "Three yards of it, you said?"

"*Jah.* That's right." She took the bundle from her friend and started unwrapping it.

"The lady at the store said this was the best material for suits and I wouldn't need three yards because the material was narrow."

Amy stopped still and stared at Lydia thinking, *What? 'Narrow' means I'd need extra, not less.*

Lydia giggled at Amy's expression. "Don't worry, I still got three yards just in case."

"You had me worried there for a minute. Don't ever do that to me again."

"I've got his measurements here too. That's what size he was a few months ago and I'm sure he hasn't changed."

"I'll make the pattern from that but before I cut it, you must bring him."

"Oh, that's not what you said the other day."

"Maybe not, but I just don't have time for mistakes."

Lydia nodded. "I'll bring him to you."

"*Gut.* Just make sure he doesn't lose weight or gain weight before the wedding."

"There isn't enough time for that."

"I hope you're right."

Lydia pointed to the tracing paper folded up on the table. "Is that the pattern over there?" She started heading in that direction.

"That's my basic suit pattern. Then I use it as my guide to cut a new one according to the measurements. Don't touch anything, whatever you do."

"My, my. You're feisty today."

"I'm always like this when I'm on a tight timeline."

"Okay. Point taken. That's why I brought you some things to help along the way."

"What do you mean?"

"*Mamm* and I made casseroles for you and Jonah because I have been so horrible in not giving you enough time to sew. I thought you could save time if you didn't have to cook."

A smile spread across Amy's face. "How kind and very thoughtful. That will save me a lot of time."

"You wait right there. I've got them in the buggy. Do you have enough room in your fridge?"

"I sure do."

While Lydia went back to her buggy, Amy hurried to her gas-powered fridge to rearrange everything to make room.

When Lydia came back, she placed a huge basket on the kitchen table. "Here we are. Three big casseroles to gobble up, two loaves of fresh bread and a dozen eggs."

"Ah, that's enough food for us for a week."

Lydia giggled. "Well, I don't know about that. I've seen how much Jonah can eat. But I do appreciate you doing the sewing."

"You're very welcome. Can you bring Lionel here tomorrow for me?"

"*Jah.*"

Amy looked up. "What's today?"

"Monday," Lydia said.

Amy shook her head. "Yeah of course it is."

"Just go ahead and use those measurements. I'm

quite confident they're correct. They were the measurements we gave to the tailor who made his suit for his *bruder's* wedding just six months ago. The suit fitted perfectly. You can blame me if I'm wrong."

"It would save time if I just went with those. Then I could start on the sewing tomorrow during the day. Then how about you bring Lionel on Wednesday evening? I should have the main components together by then."

"I'll do that."

"Good."

Lydia helped Amy put the food in the fridge.

That night, Amy tried to sleep, but she was tossing and turning and thinking about Adam. She hadn't seen him for the entire day. He hadn't mentioned he was leaving and the bishop announced on Sunday he was there for a few weeks, and Adam had said he'd be here Saturday for the wedding. She'd had to close her eyes tightly and do the best she could to put Adam out of her mind.

CHAPTER 9

AMY WOKE in the morning feeling surprisingly refreshed considering the few hours of quality sleep that she'd had. After she and Jonah ate their breakfast, she walked with Jonah to the front gate where they'd wait for Elroy, Philip and Jeff, the school-aged sons of Fay and the bishop's. Liza and her next-younger sister, Maria, had already gone past. They always walked with the Hershbergers' youngest child, Christina.

They were only there for a few minutes before the boys came racing out of the house toward Jonah.

"You all have a good day." Amy said the same thing to them every morning, and as usual the bishop's boys said they would while Jonah remained silent. He never looked back as he walked beside Elroy. When they were out of sight, she turned and saw Adam approaching.

"Where's Jonah going?"

"He's going to school."

"Oh, I didn't realize he went there."

"*Jah*, he does. I thought I mentioned something about his teacher." She shrugged. "He walks with the bishop's boys."

He shook his head. "I didn't realize. What time will he be home?"

"It depends if they come home the long or the short way. They're usually back by four."

He nodded. "Good to know."

"Well, I have work to do." She started walking to the house knowing she had a full day's work ahead of her.

"I won't hold you up. I know this must be your most valuable working time when Jonah's at school."

She stopped walking and turned around to face him. "It really is." Then she continued to the house.

LATE THAT AFTERNOON, Amy was just finishing stitching the main components of Lionel's suit jacket together when she saw Adam heading to the house with a puppy. She recalled that the bishop's dog had died a couple of years ago, and they'd never gotten another one until now. It was kind of him to bring the puppy for Jonah to see.

Then without knocking on the door, Adam sat himself down on the porch and started talking to Jonah, still with the dog in his arms.

She wasn't comfortable with somebody being around Jonah when she wasn't there, so she walked outside.

"Don't you just love him?" Adam asked Jonah; then he looked up at Amy.

Jonah looked down at the puppy, who was now out of Adam's arms and running about the porch.

Amy said, "He's adorable. I love dogs, and puppies. Is he the bishop's new dog?"

"*Nee.* I bought him for Jonah."

She looked down in horror at the puppy, pawing Jonah's legs. Jonah was still looking straight ahead.

"The puppy's for you, Jonah," Adam said.

Amy's mouth fell open and she could barely find her voice to speak. "You can't be serious."

He looked up at her, shocked. "I am. I've been doing a lot of reading at the library about children on the autism spectrum and some of them respond well to pets."

She held her throat. *A lot of research? He didn't know anything a couple of days ago.* "You spent a few minutes at the library and now you're an expert? You come here and override my authority and give Jonah a dog?" All the air left her body as the rage welled within. Silver pinpoints of light danced before her eyes and she felt she was going to faint, or have a panic attack.

"I'm sorry, but these children do well with dogs. That's what the research said."

"Well I don't! Do you think I don't have enough

work around here? I'm the *mudder,* the *vadder,* the carer, the provider and the *haus* cleaner. Do you know how much mess and how much work one puppy creates?"

"I know, but you see, the benefits would outweigh that." He picked up the puppy and put him in Jonah's lap and the dog put its paws on Jonah's shoulder and licked his face and then something completely unexpected happened. Jonah giggled. It was the first time Jonah had laughed or giggled since their parents had died.

Amy was delighted at the sound and all she could do was stare at Jonah. He had laughed! She picked up the dog and put him down on the floor of the porch. "We don't need a dog." Even though she said that, now she was torn. Perhaps a dog would be a good idea since Jonah had actually laughed. She bent down to Jonah's level. "Do you want to keep the puppy, Jonah?"

"Jah. I like him."

She stood up and looked at Adam. *"Denke,* for the dog, but I'm not happy with the way you've gone about this. You shouldn't have taken it upon yourself to decide that Jonah needs anything. I am the person who takes care of Jonah. I make the decisions for him. Can you see how this is totally inappropriate?"

Adam put his head down. "I was impulsive. I'm sorry, Amy."

"I can only think of all the mess it's going to create and how much more cleaning. With all I have to do it will create more stress in my life, and I've got as much as I can handle already and I'm way behind with everything."

"I can help," Adam said.

"You're not living here, you're visiting. You'll be gone and in my experience, people who say they'll help with something usually do so once or twice and then they don't stick around. You won't be any different."

He breathed out heavily. "I'm deeply sorry."

"And you should be. You should think before you do things."

"It was meant to be a surprise. A happy surprise, for both you and Jonah."

She looked down at the Golden Retriever puppy who was now running in circles chasing his tail. He was cute and adorable. Maybe owning a dog wouldn't be all bad.

"I can help you out financially with the dog. I've already paid in advance to have him neutered when he's older and I've paid forward for all the necessary injections, and when the time comes I'll help you. I'll take him there to get all that done while leaving you free to do your sewing work."

"That's so kind of you and such a very generous gift. I'm sorry I was so cranky. It was a lovely thought, but an animal's the kind of a surprise that isn't appropriate to be a surprise."

"I know that now." He lowered his head again. "I'm

sorry, I just wasn't thinking about the work the dog would bring."

She bit her tongue. She wanted to say, if she wanted to have a puppy she would've gone out and gotten one herself. "He must've cost you a fortune. He's full Golden Retriever by the looks."

"He is, and a gift is a gift. The receiver should not think about the price." He smiled at her and she smiled as much as she was able.

"It was kind. *Denke.*" Then she bent down, and said to Jonah, "What do you think of the new puppy, Jonah?"

"Good."

She stood up and faced Adam. "*Denke.* He says the dog is good. I guess that means we're keeping him."

"And he can accompany you on those afternoon walks."

"*Jah,* that will be nice." When they heard a buggy, they both turned to look at it. "Here are my friends, Lydia and Lionel. I'm doing the fitting for Lionel's wedding suit today. Stay and meet them. Lionel is one of the Hershbergers from next door, and Lydia is one of my best friends. Did you meet them on Sunday?"

"*Nee,* I didn't. I'll be pleased to meet them, and later I'll bring the dog's things to you. I got some food and bowls, and a cozy bed for him."

Amy felt guilty she'd been so horrible. "It was a kind thought, Adam. *Denke.*" He'd really gone to a lot of trouble and expense. A purebred Golden Retriever puppy wouldn't have come cheap and neither would the vet bills and the accessories.

After Amy introduced Adam to Lydia and Lionel, he made his excuses and left.

CHAPTER 10

AMY PUT the puppy in the laundry room with a small dish of water and plenty of newspaper, so she could concentrate on the fitting. After she washed her hands, she closed the laundry door, and was faced with Lydia in the kitchen.

"I managed to drag him here."

Lionel stepped into the kitchen. "I wouldn't say that. I know this is very important for you. For us, I should say, but I don't know why you couldn't have made it yourself," he said to Lydia.

"I could, but we're running out of time and nobody makes clothes as good as Amy. Just you wait and see."

"It's better you're here, Lionel. This way there's no room for mistakes. Follow me into the living room."

She handed pen and paper to Lydia, who wrote down the measurements as Amy called them out. All the while, Jonah was sitting on the rug in the corner playing with his rocks.

When they were done, Lydia said. "We would stay but we've so much to do."

"Where are you off to now?" Amy asked.

"We're going to make sure the wedding cakes are coming along well. We're buying some from the cake shops and then we've got two other ladies making them as well."

"I love cake," Lionel said. "That's what I look forward to at the weddings. It would be most important part if you asked me," Lionel said.

"This wedding will be something more important than cake." Lydia glared at him.

"Of course," he said with a laugh. "I'm only joking. This will be the most important day of our lives. And it will be the best day."

It made Amy happy to see her two friends so much in love. They'd all grown up together in a group and Lydia and Lionel had always been close. It made sense that they were about to marry.

AFTER LYDIA AND LIONEL LEFT, Adam came back with a large box.

"What's in it?" Amy asked opening the door for him.

"Dog food. Dry dog food. It's supposed to be good for his teeth." He set the food on the kitchen floor.

Then I've got some dog toys, a collar and a leash. I'll show Jonah how to clip on the leash."

"Okay. I'll get him."

She called Jonah into the laundry. "Adam wants to show you how to put the leash on your puppy."

Adam crouched down with Jonah and Jonah didn't watch. Instead he opened the bucket of dog food and the kibble scattered everywhere. He sat down with the food and smoothed it over and started arranging it into patterns.

"Oh, I'm so sorry, Amy," Adam said.

"Don't worry. It's not your fault."

"Shall I clean it up?"

"*Nee.* I'll have to wait until he's done." She hoped Jonah wouldn't start a new habit of playing with the dog food. Playing with stones was one thing but little pieces of dog food scattered around the place would encourage vermin.

Adam stood. "I see what you meant with what you were saying before. I've created more work for you. I'm sorry."

"Don't worry about it."

They both stood and watched Jonah create patterns and, just as he had a perfect spiral, the puppy charged through the middle and scattered the kibble everywhere. Jonah opened his mouth and squealed in frustration. Adam put his hands over his ears while Amy flew into action and pulled the dog away and closed him in the laundry room.

She crouched down beside Jonah. "The dog's away now; you can continue what you were doing." Jonah stopped squealing. She stood and signaled to Adam to join her in the living room. "See what it's like with him?" she said once they were away from Jonah.

"*Jah*. That was pretty loud."

"I know, but he doesn't usually squeal like that. He used to when he was younger, but he's pretty much grown out of it."

He sat down and she sat on the couch opposite. "I am sorry about the dog, the extra work and everything like that. I guess I was just looking at the positive side of things without seeing the negative."

"I'm the one who has to deal with the negative."

"I know. This is true."

Amy said, "I think the dog will be all right when he gets older. They are smart aren't they, these kinds of dogs?"

"That's why they're often used as companion animals and guide dogs for the blind."

"I'll train him. I guess it's hard when he's a puppy."

Adam said, "I think that's when you need to start."

"I'll have to learn how to do that." She didn't say it out loud, but she was thinking she wouldn't be able to handle one more thing. She was already at the limits of her capabilities with her sewing, trying to make an adequate income, and looking after Jonah. In between times she had to squeeze in the cooking and the cleaning.

Adam said, "I've had a lot of dogs before but I've never had to train them for someone specific like Jonah. I could try to train him for you."

At this point, she knew she could use all the help she could get. "That would be great if you could do that, but will we be taking up too much of your time?"

Adam smiled at her. "There's nothing else I'd rather be doing."

CHAPTER 11

ON THURSDAY, Amy got Jonah ready for his monthly doctor appointment. He had the day off school. Adam hadn't helped with the puppy as he'd promised and the day before he hadn't stopped by. Amy had taken the puppy on the leash to meet Jonah after school the previous day and the puppy had pulled against it, and then darted about everywhere. He clearly wasn't used to the leash, so she had to carry him. And it wasn't long after that he got heavy. Now she was cranky again about Adam giving her another living being to look after. She sure could've used some help. *He's been to the library and read up a bit about autism and now he thinks he's an expert.*

"You'll have to name the puppy soon Jonah," Amy said.

He looked up from his breakfast. "Puppy."

"You want to call him Puppy?"

"Jah."

"Okay. Puppy it is." Amy closed Puppy in the laundry room with his bed, food, and newspapers were spread over one corner of the room. He'd already learned what the newspaper was for, which was a pleasant surprise for Amy.

"Finish up your breakfast, Jonah. It's time to go."

He took another mouthful of cereal, and then carried his bowl to the sink. "I have to clean my teeth."

Amy sighed knowing he had a routine he followed for doing that, so that was another five minutes. Any other child would've forgotten and she might have said it would be okay to miss cleaning their teeth just this once. "Okay, but hurry. I'm going out to hitch the buggy; I'll meet you outside."

Just as Amy had hitched the buggy, Jonah walked outside. "Perfect timing."

He remained silent and climbed in at the same time she did. When the horse and buggy moved out of the driveway and onto the street, a distant car sped up and then crashed into the rear of the buggy, jolting them to one side.

She glanced at Jonah, who seemed unharmed, then she looked back at the car that had stopped just behind them. Amy saw a young woman driver with a cell phone in her hand. She looked just as shocked as Amy felt, and then she revved the car, zipped around them and sped away.

Amy sat there stunned until she heard Adam's

voice. "Are you okay? Amy? Jonah?" he asked sticking his head into the buggy on Jonah's side.

Amy looked again at Jonah, who didn't seem upset by the ordeal. "We're okay. You're okay aren't you, Jonah?"

"*Jah.*"

"Stay there," Adam said. "I'll check the horse." He looked over the horse and then led it off the road. "The horse seems okay, but I don't think I can say the same for the buggy."

Amy sat frozen to her seat, more shaken than she wanted to admit, and Jonah looked at her for an instant and remained silent.

"You've got a bad dent in the frame."

"Have I?" She'd never had anything like that before.

"*Jah.* I can fix it."

"*Denke.* Can I drive it into town like it is, though? We have our appointment with Dr. Janice."

"*Nee.* You can't drive this one anywhere. I'll borrow the bishop's spare and drive you in," Adam said, now standing next to her just outside the buggy.

"That's okay. We'll skip it this time. It's just a check-up. I'll call her and cancel. It was just a routine appointment."

He opened the door. "I'll take you. I've nothing else to do today and Jonah shouldn't miss an appointment. You two walk back to the *haus.*"

He was so bossy, so she didn't like to disagree. "Okay, we'll walk back, but we'll still cancel that appointment. Come on, Jonah." As they headed up the long driveway, she said, "We can't go today, Jonah. You've had a day off school for nothing. You can play with your dog for the rest of the day."

She was grateful for Adam's presence and it was handy he knew how to fix the buggy.

"I want to see Dr. Janice," Jonah said.

"Do you?" He rarely said he wanted to do anything.

"*Jah*. It's Thursday. First Thursday of the month. We need to see Dr. Janice."

That was the most she'd heard him say for a long time. "I'll ask if Adam can drive us." When Adam got the buggy back to the barn, she waited until he got out. "Adam, I've changed my mind. Would you drive us? Jonah still wants to go."

He smiled, seemingly delighted by the news. "Sure. Give me two minutes."

She turned back to Jonah. "We're going in the other buggy because something is wrong with this one." She called him over. "Come and look at this." She pointed to the large dent that was scraping against the wheel.

Jonah made no comment, and when Adam had gotten the other buggy hitched, he climbed into the backseat.

Once Amy was sitting next to Adam, she said, "*Denke* for driving us. I hope we're not interrupting your plans for the day."

"Certainly not. I like doing things for other people. I was going out in the buggy anyway."

"This is the Sunday buggy," Jonah said loudly.

"Our buggy has something wrong with it at the moment. We can't go in our buggy now." She turned away from Jonah and explained to Adam, "He only goes in the bishop's buggy on a Sunday."

"Ah, that's why he's calling it the Sunday buggy. It can also be the Thursday buggy, Jonah."

When Amy saw Jonah breathing funny and flapping his hands, she knew they weren't going anywhere that day. "We'll have to turn back now, Adam."

He glanced over at her. "What do you mean?"

"We'll have to go back. He's upset."

"But you have an appointment and he was all right a moment ago."

She shook her head and hoped Adam wasn't going to be stubborn about the sudden change of plans. She was used to that, but Adam wasn't. He might see it as Jonah being disobedient. "It doesn't matter. We can't go when he's this upset. He will just get worse."

He stopped the buggy, turned around and headed back.

Amy faced Jonah. "It's okay. We're going back home now."

Adam was getting a taste of what it was like caring for Jonah.

"What will you do about the appointment?" asked Adam.

"I'll call them when we get back. We'll just skip this one. It won't matter, not really."

Adam nodded. "Okay. I'll take a look at that buggy for you."

"*Denke.*"

He glanced behind at Jonah who had calmed down a little now that they were heading home. "Will he be okay?"

"Yeah, he'll be fine."

Jonah calmed down when he saw they were going back home.

When they got back, Adam said, "I don't have tools with me and the bishop doesn't have the ones I need. Someone around here must them. I'll find out who and I'll be back."

"*Denke.* I appreciate this very much."

"It'll be as good as new. Don't worry about a thing. I do this for a living. Not repairing, but I work on buggies and I've done my share of repairs, too." He chuckled while he guided her by her arm. "Now you go back inside and don't worry."

"Okay."

THROUGHOUT THE DAY, she left Jonah sitting on the porch with the puppy on a long leash beside him, and she continued sewing. She saw Adam head off in the bishop's buggy and he was gone for some time.

When he arrived back, he headed straight to the barn and didn't come to see her. She knew he'd gotten those tools because he hadn't come out and she heard him working on the buggy.

As a blanket of darkness fell over the house, Jonah and Amy ate their evening meal, and there were still noises coming from the barn. "He's still out there working. I'll take him a meal." She took him a plate of food and then saw Fay hurrying away with a tray. Amy entered the barn to see him stooped over the buggy and looking thoughtful. "Are you still working?"

He looked up at her, hammer in hand. "It's not quite as straightforward as I hoped, but I'll get there." He went back to tinkering with it.

"Have you eaten?" She held up the plate. "I brought you dinner."

"Ah, *denke*. But Fay brought me some and I just ate it."

"I feel so bad putting you to all this trouble."

"Nonsense. I'm happy to be helping out." He straightened up and stared at her. "I'll come and see you in the morning and give you an update on it."

"Okay."

"*Gut nacht*, Amy."

"*Gut nacht*." She turned around and walked away with the plate of food.

When she was trying to sleep late that night, she could still hear faint noises from the barn. Or was she imagining them?

CHAPTER 12

ADAM WALKED UP to her as she was seeing Jonah off to school.

"It's fixed."

"Oh, great. *Denke.* I hope you got some sleep."

"Jah, I got enough."

The bishop's boys ran up to Jonah.

"Bye, boys. Have a good day," Amy called out as they started walking.

"We will, bye," Elroy called out.

They watched the boys for a moment, and then Adam said, "I think we should test it out."

She was still watching Jonah and the boys walking up the road. "The buggy?"

"Jah."

She had sewing waiting for her, but she couldn't say no, especially seeing as he'd worked on it for so many hours. *"Jah,* if it can be quick. Otherwise it'll have to wait. I've got so much work waiting for me."

"A quick ten minutes is all we'll need."

"Okay good. I appreciate it. Can we just wait until they're out of sight?"

"Sure."

"I usually stand here and wait until I can't see them anymore."

When the boys were gone, Amy followed Adam to the barn and watched as he hitched the buggy to the horse. He did it so much faster than she was able.

"After you," he said when he led the horse out onto the driveway.

She gave a little giggle as she got up into the buggy. "Where are we off to?"

He climbed in after her. "Just up the road and back. I would've suggested we do something today but it's difficult with you working too."

"I know. I don't get much free time." She held onto the side of the buggy when they came to the spot where the car had run into them.

"You okay?" he asked.

"Just a little nervous now. It really shook me up. I've never had that happen to me before."

He shook his head. "Something should be done. Car drivers don't respect buggies enough. They go far too close. Either that, or they grow impatient and try to pass when there's oncoming traffic."

"I've noticed that."

He tipped his hat back slightly on his head. "Anyway, I shouldn't grumble. How's the buggy feeling?"

"Smooth. Thanks so much."

He drove to the end of the road and then turned around. "Not a car in sight today."

"Good."

He delivered her back to her front door. "There you are, back to work safe and sound."

"I appreciate it."

"If you need anything at all, just ask. How is the dog?"

"Good. Jonah named him Puppy."

"Oh, I see. That's original."

"That's Jonah." She climbed down. "I'll see you later."

"Have a good day."

"*Denke.*" She walked inside and from her sewing desk, she watched as he unhitched the buggy. When she heard scratching in the laundry, she remembered Puppy. She opened the laundry door and Puppy sprang at her wagging his whole body and not just his tail. "Hello there; I wasn't gone that long." She clipped the leash on him and took him out the laundry room door on the other side of the house so Adam wouldn't see her.

CHAPTER 13

It was late morning on Friday when she saw Adam walking to the house with a white cardboard box in his hands. This time she didn't mind the interruption because she was just about to have a break from her work. She opened the door to see his smiling face.

"How are you?"

"Great. I've just been into town and I bought doughnuts." He opened the lid and she saw brightly-colored iced doughnuts.

"That's very nice of you, but Tabitha has Jonah on a strict diet. He is off all processed and glutinous foods."

"Who said they're for Jonah?"

She laughed at the twinkle in his eyes. "For me?"

"They could be."

"Well, I hope you'll have one too."

"*Jah*, if you'll make me a cup of *kaffe*."

"Sure."

He nodded. "Why don't we sit out on the porch?"

"Okay. I'll be back soon with the *kaffe*."

A few minutes later, she brought out two cups of coffee and placed them on the table between the two chairs. As he sipped his coffee, she took her cup in her hand and imagined that they were a married couple sitting down taking time out of their day to enjoy each other's company while the *kinner* were in school. She closed her eyes and enjoyed the gentle cool breeze on her skin. "It's such a beautiful day. I didn't even need to put the fire on this morning."

"Let me know if you need me to chop wood for you."

"*Denke*, but the bishop shares his wood with me and his oldest son has the chore of chopping it." She smiled at him. It was nice having a man around, but she wouldn't get too used to it.

"Where's Puppy?"

"Fast asleep. Shhh. Don't wake him. I'm enjoying the quiet time. I can't leave work on the floor anymore, everything has to be up on the table."

He flipped the lid of the box open and pushed it toward her. "Have one."

She stared at the mouth-watering array of multi-colored frosted doughnuts. In her head, she heard Tabitha telling her not to have one. "I don't usually eat things like this, but they do look good." She looked into his blue-green eyes. "Will you have one?"

"I sure will."

She took a pink one and bit into it and, as she chewed, it melted in her mouth. "I haven't had anything quite so good in some time."

"Is it really necessary that you take him to Tabitha for all that when he's seeing a doctor?"

She stared at him shocked. He might as well have called what Tabitha did nonsense. "Doctors are good at treating ailments, but a herbalist works on the overall health of a person and, hopefully the causes of poor health."

"You're not saying you think Tabitha can heal him, are you? Because from what I've read —"

She shrugged her shoulders. "I honestly don't think there is a cure. Jonah is that way to stay. That's how he is. Anyway, Tabitha hasn't had any official training, but a lot of people go to her when they're sick rather than going to a doctor. I figure anything that helps Jonah feel more comfortable in his skin is worth doing."

He nodded. "That's right. I forgot she did all that. I know you've told me before that you take Jonah to see her, but I knew before that she did that. *Mamm* said Tabitha's mother had studied all that, too."

"She knows what she's doing."

"How did Jonah come to get this ... disorder, if that's what it's called?"

"Nobody knows what causes it. There are a few different theories, but no one knows for sure."

"How often does he see his doctor?"

"Every month. And he sees Tabitha about the same. Although Tabitha comes here."

"So, on a school day he doesn't have a three o'clock walk?"

"*Nee.* That's only for Saturday and Sunday. We don't have a walk when he comes home from school because he's done enough walking by then."

"It must be hard on you looking after him."

She took a deep breath. "I feel like I've been doing it alone my whole life. It's definitely been harder since both of our parents have gone and it's just Jonah and me."

"But, you do have the support of everybody in the community."

"I do. And I'm grateful for that. Everyone knows what he's like now and they just accept him. Jonah is how he is, and that's that. Even at school, everyone's really good with him." She stared at him. "Why are you here, Adam?"

"I came to bring Jonah doughnuts." He laughed a little.

"I'm not talking about that. Why are you here in this community right now?"

"Oh." He chuckled. "Well, it's a long story. It was my parents' idea, not mine."

They were distracted by Fay walking toward them. "There you are, Adam. Morgan's been looking for you."

He jumped to his feet. "Coming."

Amy stood up and closed the box of doughnuts. "Take this with you."

Adam shook his head. *"Nee,* you eat them."

"I couldn't. I don't normally eat this kind of food and besides there's way too many."

He took the box from her outstretched hands. "Okay, I'll give them to Fay's *kinner,"* he whispered. "Would you be okay if I came back and asked Jonah to go fishing with me and Elroy tomorrow morning?"

"I think that would be lovely."

Adam gave her a big smile and then he walked off with Fay. Adam had said it was his parents' idea he was there. Her best guess was they wanted him to find a wife and maybe he wasn't so interested. He certainly was showing a lot of empathy toward Jonah. Maybe a man like him might be okay for her. For the first time, she could see that getting married was a possibility. She'd never thought a man would take the time to know Jonah.

WHEN AMY'S alarm sounded telling her it was time to wait for Jonah by the fence, she clipped Puppy's leash on him and together they walked down to the road. She hoped that Adam would come out and say hello, but there was no sign of him.

When the boys came into view, she picked Puppy up and tried to show him that the boys were coming. Puppy didn't know what she was doing and kept turning his head trying to bite her hands. She placed him down on the ground, and like they usually did, the boys ran the last twenty yards home. The boys all leaned down to pet Puppy, all of them except Jonah who stood there with a pleasant look on his face, which was almost a smile.

Fay soon called her boys inside to do their after-school chores, and Amy and Jonah continued to their house with Puppy trying to bite and play with the leash all the way.

CHAPTER 14

On Saturday morning when Amy saw Adam approaching the house, she opened the door and he smiled at her. "I've come to talk with Jonah."

Amy nodded.

"Jonah, would you like to go fishing with me and three of the bishop's boys?" He glanced at Amy. "If it's okay with Amy."

Jonah shook his head.

Adam stepped forward. "Oh, come on, Jonah. You don't have to fish; you can just sit there and watch us. We're walking to the river and you like walking, don't you?"

"*Jah*." Jonah said.

Adam looked up at Amy for help as he sat on the top step. "Will he go?"

"Do you want to go to the river with them, Jonah? I'll come too."

"Jah."

Amy was pleased that he was doing something different. Something out of his normal routine. But as much as she was pleased, she was also wary. What if he got down to the river and had one of his panic attacks?

"That would be *wunderbaar.* I'll get everything ready and meet you back here in fifteen minutes."

"Okay." As Adam hurried off, Amy said, "Come on, Jonah, you'll have to dress warmly, and we'll take Puppy with us."

Soon the three of the bishop's school-age sons, Jeff, Elroy, and Philip, were back along with Adam. The four boys set off walking to the river.

Amy walked behind them with Adam, who was carrying most of the fishing gear. "Thank you for taking the time to do this with them," Amy said, pulling Puppy by his leash as he was trying to smell everything rather than walk.

"I love doing things like this with children. I'm just a big kid myself really. I've never grown-up."

She giggled. She wished her life had been like that but she'd had to grow up and become an adult fast because of her brother. "If you haven't grown up now, when you think you'll grow up?"

He chuckled. "It could be years and maybe never. I don't think people really grow up. I think everyone's a child inside and we are just acting like adults. We've learned how to pretend we're adults but inside, deep down, nothing really changes. We just get more knowledge. But that doesn't change who we are inside."

"I see you've given this a lot of thought."

"I do think a lot about things. I know you wouldn't be able to tell that from how I acted the first time we met."

"That's true, very true. You seemed like a man who didn't think at all. Or just did the first thing that came into your mind."

He shook his head. "You told me not to apologize about that again otherwise I would."

"Please don't. It's getting old."

He smiled as he shifted the fishing gear to his other arm. "Have you done much fishing before?"

"Not really. I don't like fishing or hunting or anything like that. I prefer to buy my food all ready to cook and preferably packaged." She giggled. "I'm joking, but I don't like my food looking at me."

He chuckled. "You've never taken Jonah fishing before?"

She shook her head. "Why? Is that unusual?"

"*Nee,* but I can't imagine growing up without going fishing."

"We didn't grow up doing that kind of thing. I think I was always in the kitchen with my mother or we were sewing together. And when Jonah came along, he was different from all of the other boys."

"When did anyone notice Jonah was different?"

"*Mamm* said it was when he was a few months old. He just didn't make eye contact or reach the same milestones as most children. My *mudder* took him to the clinic and that's when he was diagnosed as being on the autism spectrum."

"You're doing a remarkable job with your *bruder.*"

It made her feel good that he said that. "*Denke.* I try to do a good job. He deserves that."

"He does." He called out to the boys not to get too far ahead and then they slowed down.

Instead of struggling with Puppy, she reached down and picked him up.

"Is he heavy?" Adam asked.

She changed the dog's position. "He is, a little, and he's wiggly."

"Do you want to swap, and you take the fishing rods?"

"Okay."

He placed the rods down on the ground and she passed Puppy over and picked up the rods; then they continued walking, a little faster now because the boys were getting further ahead again.

"We should be wearing him out, that's what we should be doing, so he'll sleep later," Adam said regarding Puppy.

"There's no problem about him sleeping. He sleeps most of the day anyway. And it's not enjoyable to take him on a walk until he learns to lead properly. He keeps pulling or dawdling."

"I'm sorry I haven't been around to train him. The bishop's had me doing odd jobs for people. Not that I mind, but I wasn't given any notice. I hope I can spend some time with him tomorrow. I've had plenty of dogs before so I know what I'm doing." He looked over at her. "You look worried."

Amy laughed. "I didn't realize I was looking worried."

"It must be a habit, then."

"I hope not. I don't want to be going around for the rest of my life looking worried."

Amy wondered what it would be like to have children of her own and to be walking to the river with them to go fishing. "What do you do in the bishop's *haus* all day, Adam?"

"I'm not in the *haus* all day. I've been out and about, going here and there doing odd jobs for people. The bishop's put me to work."

Amy chuckled. "I'm sorry, you just told me that."

"*Jah.*"

"Did you think you were coming here for a rest or something?"

"I was kind of hoping to get a breather."

"The bishop is very driven and he has a lot of energy. He doesn't stop and neither does Fay. They're always helping people. Just like they helped me and Jonah with a place to live."

"Where were you living before that?"

"In our own *haus*. It wasn't in good repair, though,

so that's why the bishop moved us here and then some of the men in the community fixed it. I'm just waiting on some plumbing to be done and then we'll be able to move back in." She neglected to tell him that the plumbing costs were huge and she was saving and working hard to get the water connected back to the house. She wouldn't accept the bishop's idea of a fundraiser for them.

Amy had half the money saved and it wouldn't take long for her to make up the rest of the money. The only thing she was worried about was Jonah's transition back to their old place. Would it bring back memories of their parents?

She was sure her brother had taken it hard when they died, and to move back into the same house might bring back a sudden flood of memories. They couldn't live in the bishop's house forever. He'd need it for other people in bad circumstances.

"You've gone very quiet, Amy."

"I do that sometimes. I just start thinking about one thing and then it leads to another and another."

"What was it that you were thinking about?"

She ended up telling him about her problem with the plumbing, and raising the money, and the issue of Jonah moving back into their old house.

"I think you're right. It might be too much for Jonah to go back there."

"It would be convenient if he was okay with it, but the other problem I have is he likes everything constant all the time, without change, and now he's gotten used to living here at the bishop's place."

"Couldn't that be a permanent arrangement?"

"I don't think the bishop ever meant it to be permanent."

"You've been here awhile now, haven't you?"

She nodded. "I have. Every time I bring it up they say to stay here with them. They won't even take a regular rent. But I do pay them a little every week."

"Something will work out. It always does."

"You're right. My *vadder* used to say that half the things—more than half the things we worry about never actually happen."

"Sounds like you were a worrier for a long time."

"I think that's something I got from my *mudder*. She was a worrier too."

He nodded. "I think most women are and they cry a lot."

"I never cry," Amy said. "I don't know why, but no matter how bad things got, I never cried."

The boys squealed because they had reached the river.

"Here we are," the bishop's eldest son, Philip said. They rushed back to Adam and Amy to fetch their fishing rods.

"Hey, don't scare the fish," Adam said. "I've got some old meat to put on those hooks. I don't know how we'll catch any fish with that, but we'll try."

While they set about fussing over their rods and

hooks, Amy sat on the bank with Jonah and Puppy, watching everyone. She was pleased Jonah looked interested in what they were doing.

96

CHAPTER 15

A MY HAD GOTTEN a few hours of sewing done that afternoon once they were back from fishing. Then a buggy pulled up. She looked up to see whether it was a visitor for her or the bishop. It was her good friend, Sarah. Amy dropped her sewing, ran to the door, flung it open and ran toward her. Sarah jumped down from the buggy and the two girls hugged.

"Come inside and tell me everything that you've been doing. I can't believe you were away for so long. I think your *mudder* was a little upset that you decided to stay the extra week."

"I met someone and couldn't tell *Mamm*. Not just yet."

"Really?"

Sarah nodded enthusiastically.

"I met someone too."

The girls giggled, and Sarah said, "You'll have to tell

SAMANTHA PRICE

me all about him. And I brought healthy cookies. *Mamm* made them. I'll get them." She grabbed the bag of cookies and then linked arms with Amy as they walked toward the house.

"Hello, Jonah," Sarah said, and was seemingly ignored, but that was the usual way. Jonah rarely spoke to Amy's friends.

Once they were inside, Sarah flopped down on the couch.

"Do you want a drink or anything?" Amy asked.

"*Nee,* I'll just have a cookie. Sit down with me and we can talk about our men. Shall I go first?"

"*Jah,* you go first and you must tell me everything about him."

Sarah opened the bag of cookies. "Here. Take a couple out to Jonah and hurry back."

"Okay." Amy grabbed two cookies and took them out to Jonah, who accepted them without hesitation. Then the two girls sat in front of the crackling fire nibbling on cookies.

Sarah began, "He's so lovely. We got on immediately. It was love at first sight for me, and I'm sure it was the same for him. I've never met anyone who suited me so well."

"I'm so happy for you." Amy was eating the cookie slowly because it didn't taste the best. Nothing close to as good as the doughnuts Adam had brought over. "And is he handsome?"

The smile left Sarah's face to be replaced by a

thoughtful expression. "He's okay to look at, but it was his personality that attracted me. He's a little bit shorter than I'd like. I've always wanted a tall man, but at least he's taller than I am."

"Everyone's taller than you," Amy joked.

Sarah giggled. "That's true. He is a dairy farmer. His family has a lot of land besides the pastures for the cows, and they grow soybeans and other things. I forget what. He's got a big family and he has no brothers, only sisters, five of them. He's the oldest. Now I've told you the best part; next I will tell you the worst."

"What? Does he already have a girlfriend?"

"*Nee,* it's nothing to do with him. It's my folks. They want me to marry someone else."

Amy screwed up her face. "How can that be?"

"It was talked about amongst the families over the years, but I never thought it would really happen, but now I find out they're serious and Adam's parents have sent him here to propose."

Amy nearly stopped breathing and the room felt like it was spinning around. Her Adam? Then everything made sense like the pieces of a jigsaw puzzle fitting together. That was why Adam was there and that was why he didn't want to say why he was there. She coughed a couple of times in an effort to hide her shock. "Do you mean Adam Brown, the one who's staying here with the bishop?"

"That's the one. We've met before, and he's okay, but I'm not in love with him. Far from it. I want to marry someone I'm in love with. Otherwise, what's the point?"

Amy wasn't pleased to hear that about Adam. She stared at the flickering flames in the fireplace wondering what to say and trying to hide her disappointment.

"Who did you meet? Tell me everything from the time you first met."

Amy looked back at her friend. "What?"

"Tell me about the man you met."

Amy was still in shock. "Oh. I did meet someone new, but it's not a man." Amy was feeling sick to the stomach, feeling like a fool. "I'll show you who I met. Come with me." She took Sarah into the laundry room and showed her the puppy. She'd pretend it was the pup she'd been talking about and Sarah wouldn't know any different. Sarah let out a squeal of delight when the puppy came bounding toward them. She sank down on the floor and hugged him.

"He's gorgeous."

Amy sat down too. "I know."

"Oh, Amy, what will I do about my parents wanting me to marry Adam?"

"Tell them how you feel."

Sarah scoffed. "I don't think they care how I feel."

"You're a grown woman. You make your own choices."

"I still can't go against what they say."

"Have they met your man you like so much?"

"*Nee*. They haven't. His name's Elijah."

"Isn't that the first thing you should do?" Amy asked.

"How would I arrange that?"

"Arrange for him to visit and stay with someone in the community the same as Adam's staying at the bishop's."

"You're a genius, Amy."

"I'm hardly a genius; it's kind of obvious."

"It's worth a try. Anything's worth a try. Have you met Adam?"

Amy nodded. "*Jah*, he's been here for about a week now. I think that's why your parents felt upset you didn't come home when you were supposed to."

"Well, I'm glad I didn't. What's Adam like? Tell me more about him. I don't know him because I haven't seen him since I was a kid."

"He's nice, and he's very thoughtful. He's been good to Jonah and he also took Jonah, Puppy and the bishop's boys fishing this morning."

"What made you get this little guy?"

She had to think fast. "I heard it would be good for Jonah. Did I tell you he named him Puppy?"

Sarah laughed. "That's a typical thing for Jonah to do. That's really funny."

The girls watched the puppy darting about with one of his toys in his mouth. Amy didn't tell her Adam had given Jonah the puppy because it was an expensive gift, and she didn't want any problems with anyone. She'd learned a long time ago that trouble happened when people talked too much. Best she keep her mouth shut.

"The first day he got Puppy was the first time I heard him laugh since our parents died. And then he's laughed at him two more times this week."

"It sounds like the dog is doing Jonah some good."

Amy nodded. "He is."

"And how is Jonah doing other than that?"

"I was taking him to the doctor on Thursday and a car crashed into us just at the bottom of the driveway. Adam offered to drive us there in the bishop's buggy and then Jonah started having a panic attack."

"Oh dear. Was he waving his arms about?"

"He was. So, we turned around and came back home."

"Was your buggy damaged?"

"It was, but Adam managed to fix it. I found out that's what he does for a living."

"Has he been spending a bit of time with you?"

"Not really." She bit the inside of her lip not wanting to lie. "Maybe a little bit. He seems quite nice." She was relieved that Sarah was in love with someone else, but nothing was definite until Sarah was set to marry the other man. With her parents never having met him, that might take some time. "Are you going to talk to Elijah about coming here to meet your folks? Maybe if your parents meet him, they'll see how you two feel about each other."

"I think I have to. I see that as the only way

anything can happen between us, especially now that Adam's in the way. I have to let *Mamm* see that I don't care for Adam."

"What about your *vadder*?"

Sarah shrugged. "It's *Mamm* who's the driving force trying to get me married. *Dat* just goes along with her."

Amy recalled what Adam had said. She thought Sarah would feel better knowing that. "He did tell me he was here because it was his parents' idea."

"Are you saying he doesn't love me?"

Amy gulped, not expecting that reaction. "Did you expect him to? I thought you'd only met a couple of times."

"But, all the same, I expected him to like me if he came here to see me. Otherwise, it's rude."

"But it's your parents. You said it was your *mudder* who wanted this. Are you starting to have doubts about Elijah?"

"I'm not having doubts about him." Puppy bounced into Sarah's lap making her giggle. "He's adorable. I want to take him home."

"How about we take him outside on the leash?"

"Okay."

Amy was pleased that Puppy had interrupted them. The conversation had been heading into dangerous territory. She clipped the leash onto Puppy's collar and together she and Sarah headed out of the house. When they were outside, all Sarah could talk about, right up until the time she left, was Elijah.

CHAPTER 16

AMY WAS ENJOYING snuggling up in a soft blanket as she sat on the porch with Jonah on the lazy Sunday morning. The cool air was nipping at her face and she pulled the blanket up higher. Since the church gatherings were held every other Sunday, today was their day off, but still their day of rest. Amy was determined to make the most of it and not think about work, or deadlines, or Adam.

The only thing was, she couldn't stop her mind from wandering to Adam. Since Sarah had come back yesterday, she hadn't seen him at all. She'd seen him leave early that morning and he still hadn't returned. From nearly every window of the house, except the kitchen, she was able to watch the movements of whoever came and went. Where was he? Was he out visiting Sarah's parents? She thought that was most likely where he was.

When darkness fell that evening, she saw Adam return. From the couch, she noticed he didn't even glance over at her place. Something had changed between them she could feel it.

WHEN AMY'S alarm sounded Monday afternoon, she left off her sewing, clipped on Puppy's leash and headed down to the front gate to meet Jonah.

As she waited, she could hear footsteps behind her, but didn't turn around.

"Hey there."

She turned around, knowing to whom the male voice belonged. "Hello, Adam."

"What are you doing?"

It was an odd thing to say because he knew what she was doing there. Was he nervous? Or was he feeling odd because he had liked her until he met Sarah? What if Sarah liked him, too? "I'm waiting for the children to come home from school." The best way, she felt was to have everything out in the open. "Sarah visited me on Saturday. That's why you're here, for Sarah?"

"You know?"

Amy nodded. "She told me all about it."

He stepped closer to her. "I haven't agreed to anything yet. My parents were adamant that I come here to at least see Sarah once again. That's all I agreed to. They have in mind we should marry."

"And how do you feel now you've seen her again?"

"She didn't say anything, but I feel she's just as reluctant about this whole thing as I am."

She bit her lip. She couldn't tell him about Elijah and him being the reason Sarah had stayed extra time in Walnut Creek. "I suppose she just wants to make her own choice."

"I can understand that." He reached down and patted Puppy. "How's Puppy doing?"

"Just as I thought. He's a lot of work."

He chuckled and stood up. "But what about Jonah?"

"Jonah loves him. Who wouldn't love a puppy?"

"You, apparently."

"I'm getting attached to him, but as I told you …"

"I know, I know. A lot of work and a lot of mess, but hopefully the rewards will outweigh all that."

She looked up to the end of the road. "Ah, here they come now."

"What happens in the rain? How do they get home?"

"Fay collects them in the buggy."

"And Jonah doesn't mind the change of routine?"

"That's the routine for when there's rain, so that's okay."

"Got it."

There was no denying that there was something

between them. She could tell he liked her, too, but now the whole thing was awkward with Sarah and the reason he'd come there. Even if nothing came of it, Adam had made her see that it might be possible to have someone in her life and eventually marry somebody. And maybe with two incomes, she could work a little less frantically. It was hard being the sole breadwinner of her small family of two. *"Denke* for fixing my buggy the other day."

"It was nothing for me. There was nothing complicated and I do that kind of thing all the time." He stared over at the children. "I would like to do something nice for Jonah. Is there anything I can do?"

"I can't think of anything."

"What kind of things does he like? I know he likes to go for walks and he collects things along the way. That's all he seems to like, as well as Puppy. I'm not sure if he enjoyed the fishing the other day, but I think it was good for him to try something different."

"I agree. It was."

"Does he collect anything besides rocks?"

"Sometimes small sticks and at night if he's awake he arranges them in his room in patterns. You've seen him do something like that. Remember when Puppy ruined his design with the dry dog-food pieces?"

He laughed. "I do remember. Is there anything else?"

"Not really. He's not coordinated enough to play ball games with the other children. I don't know, maybe something involving science or something he can learn. He seems to prefer that rather than doing physical things. Anyway, I'm guessing you'll be busy with Sarah and her family for the next few days now that Sarah's back?"

He shrugged his shoulders. "I saw them nearly all day yesterday."

She noticed that wasn't an answer, and she was right about where he'd been yesterday.

When the boys reached them, the bishop's children begged Adam to take them fishing again. Adam knew they all had chores before and after school, and told them he might possibly take them all again next Saturday. Amy reminded them that Saturday was the wedding.

CHAPTER 17

WHEN TUESDAY MORNING CAME, Amy had to find out what was going on between Sarah and Adam. She could feel herself falling for him and she had to put a stop to it if Sarah liked him. She'd been up extra early sewing to make up the time she'd be away that day, and as soon as Jonah left for school, she headed to Sarah's house.

JUST AS SHE was securing the buggy, Tabitha, Sarah's mother, came hurrying over, tossing a shawl about her shoulders.

"Did Sarah tell you about Adam?"

She stared at Tabitha, who seemed flustered. The woman hadn't even said hello. "*Jah,* she told me you want her to marry him. Is that right?"

Tabitha laughed. "We're not forcing her, but we're having him to dinner tonight and we'll see how the two of them hit it off. He spent most of Sunday here and if I'm not wrong, they'll be married soon."

Amy breathed out heavily. "So, there's been no actual marriage arranged?"

"*Nee*. We're hoping they will marry. They're perfect for one another. They even look good together."

"I hope the dinner goes well for you."

"The reason I've come out of the *haus* to meet you away from Sarah's ears is that she's starting to babble about somebody she met while she was visiting her aunt. Did she mention anything to you about him?"

"Who?" she asked, preferring not to talk about it. She'd be betraying Sarah's confidence.

"His name is Elijah something or other. She likes him."

"She did mention something about him."

"What did she say exactly?" Tabitha peered into her face.

"I was a bit distracted at the time, so I don't think I was listening very well. What did she tell you?"

"She mentioned the word love. It's so easy for the young to fall in love, and I know nothing about this man. Sometimes the person who pulls your heart might not be the same person who you'd be better off with."

"That makes sense."

"Does it?" Tabitha asked searching Amy's eyes.

"*Jah*, it does." Amy nodded for extra emphasis.

"I wish Sarah would see things the way you do. You're so mature for your age."

Amy smiled at Tabitha. She'd had no choice but to grow up fast. But she wasn't that mature, all she was doing was agreeing with Tabitha and that amused Amy. "Adam does seem nice. He's very kind. Did you know he bought …"

Tabitha leaned forward. "*Jah?*"

She thought it best not to tell Sarah's mother Adam had bought Jonah a puppy. "He brought over some doughnuts the other day."

"*Ach nee*, you didn't give Jonah any, did you?"

"Fortunately, Jonah was at school and I gave them back to Adam to give to Fay's *kinner*. Jonah didn't even get to see them."

She patted Amy on the back. "That's good. Have you been keeping him on the diet?"

"I've followed your diet plan to the letter."

"And has he been taking the magnesium and the fish oil supplements?"

Amy said, "He's had them every day."

"Good. Sarah's upstairs."

Amy made her way through the house and knocked on Sarah's bedroom door.

"Come in?" Sarah said, as she was finishing off making her bed. "Oh, it's you. I thought it was *Mamm*. I didn't even hear your buggy."

Amy sat on the end of her friend's newly made bed.

"I needed a break and thought I'd come see you. I really missed you when you were away."

Sarah sat down with her. "Adam's coming to dinner. It's tonight or tomorrow night. I forget."

"Your *Mamm* said it's tonight."

"Oh. She's going to want me to cook it, so I can impress him with my skills."

"How do you like him now that you've met him?"

"I would've really liked him if I hadn't already met Elijah. He's nothing like Elijah, they're so different. Adam is kind and gentle and Elijah is more loud and outrageous."

"Outrageous?"

Sarah giggled. "Kind of silly. He's only like that with me. I'm not looking forward to this dinner."

"It won't be that bad. He seems very nice."

"I don't want nice."

"But isn't Elijah nice?"

"He's nice to me," Sarah said.

Amy giggled. "That's a relief. You had me worried for a minute."

"Oh, Amy, you know I wouldn't like anybody who wasn't nice. I'm just worried about this. Why do these things happen to me all the time? You're lucky you're free to do whatever you want."

"Only because my parents aren't here anymore. But with Jonah, it's not true that I'm free. I always have to consider his needs as he has no one else."

"Oh, I didn't mean to make you upset."

Amy shook her head. "You didn't. It's just how my life is. Have you made any commitments to Elijah?"

"*Nee,* I haven't."

"I should go. I only stopped by briefly. I hope you get through the dinner."

"Me too. I'll call over tomorrow and tell you how it went."

Amy stood up. "Okay."

"Do you need to leave so soon?"

"*Jah,* I do," Amy said. "Work is waiting."

Sarah sighed. "*Denke* for stopping by. I'll walk outside with you. Then I'll have to start cooking this amazing dinner we're having tonight." Sarah rolled her eyes, which made Amy giggle.

THAT NIGHT as Jonah and Amy ate their evening meal, Amy couldn't stop wondered how Sarah and Adam were getting along.

Adam had said he'd train Puppy, but so far, he hadn't done much. Even so, Puppy was getting used to his leash and starting to obey a few commands—come, and sit, and lie down when he wasn't excited or distracted.

Amy tried to wait up to see what time Adam came home, but she fell asleep too early. The last time she remembered looking at the clock it was ten minutes to eleven and he still wasn't back. That had to mean he was having a good time.

CHAPTER 18

WHEN AMY RETURNED to the house after watching Jonah leave for school, she sat down and started right in on her sewing, hoping Sarah wouldn't forget to stop by. She was aching to know how the dinner had gone.

It was twelve o'clock when Sarah's buggy pulled up outside her door. Amy flung the door open and waited for her to approach.

"Well, how was it?" Amy asked in a quiet voice so she couldn't be heard just in case anyone was about.

Sarah shrugged her shoulders and walked over. "It was okay."

"I'll make us a cup of hot tea and a sandwich. I was just about to stop for lunch."

As they sat down with the sandwiches and their cups of tea, there was a knock on the door.

Amy looked out. "It's him."

"Adam?"

"*Jah.*"

"What's he doing here?" Sarah whispered.

"He visits from time to time to ask questions about Jonah."

"Quick go see what he wants."

Amy opened the door. "Hello, Adam."

"Hi. Is that Sarah's buggy?"

"*Jah*, it is. We were just having a sandwich and a cup of tea. Would you like to join us?"

She was hoping he wouldn't because Sarah hadn't even told her how the dinner went. He immediately took off his hat and a hint of a smile appeared at the corners of his lips. Right then she knew she'd lost him to one of her best friends.

"I'd love to," he said.

Amy stepped back and opened the door wider. "The kitchen is just there through to the right." He walked through to the kitchen and greeted Sarah.

"We are just having tuna sandwiches if that's all right with you?"

"That'll be fine."

As she made more sandwiches, she said, "And you two had dinner last night I believe?"

"We did. It was a good night," Adam said. He looked over at Amy. "How's Jonah today?"

"He's good," Amy said.

"No more episodes like he had in the buggy the other day?"

She glanced over and could feel Sarah's disapproval

at Adam paying her too much attention.

"*Nee*. And he's responding well to Puppy."

"That's good."

"I'm teaching him to put the leash on the dog and take him out when he heads to the door."

"That's excellent. I know I said I'd train him and I will. I've just been distracted."

Amy looked up and saw Sarah and Adam smiling at one another. "You don't have to train him. I'm pretty sure I can do it. He's already good now on the leash. And Jonah is leading him nicely on our walks. I still have to watch both of them though."

"Jonah must be such a burden on you," Sarah said.

"He's not a burden. I'm glad to have him. We're a team."

"But if he was normal, then things would be so much easier for you."

"*Gott* didn't want him to be like everybody else," Adam said, now flashing a smile at Amy.

"I think you're right, Adam. He's special and that's just how *Gott* wants him to be." Amy shrugged. "And I can't complain about that."

Sarah continued, "Yeah, I know but there's all the doctor's appointments and all the worries that he'll be upset over things."

Amy placed a plate of food in front of Adam, wondering why her friend was saying all these things. She'd never been negative about Jonah like that before.

"I'm sorry that this is all I have for lunch. If I had

known I was having visitors, I would have had something more elaborate."

"This is fine. This is lovely. I like tuna sandwiches and I don't often get them."

"You knew I was coming," Sarah said with a laugh. "I'm not as important as Adam?"

Amy sat down not knowing what to say. "I'm just making excuses, then, I guess."

Adam laughed and Sarah laughed along with him.

The three of them sat there in silence for what seemed like several minutes, but it was probably only one. The whole thing with the two of them being there was awkward and complicated. And the way Sarah kept staring at Adam, Amy was more than certain that she had forgotten all about Elijah. The silence continued. They certainly couldn't talk about their two sets of parents expecting them to marry, not in front of her.

"And how do you like our community, Adam?" Sarah asked.

"I like it. I've been here before, a couple of times when I was younger."

"Oh, I didn't know that," Amy said, before she realized he'd told her already.

"I don't have much memory of it myself. I was told I came here and that's all I know."

"And you were in Walnut Creek recently, Sarah," Adam said.

"That's right. I was there visiting one of my aunts."

"And did you like it?"

"Very much so. I could live there."

Amy was more than glad the lunch was over, and Adam excused himself.

"What did he come here for?" Sarah asked.

"I'm not entirely sure. He pops over from time to time."

Sarah glared at Amy from across the table. "You've got a mad crush on him, haven't you?"

"*Nee*, I haven't." Amy stood up and started clearing the plates from the table.

"You have. I can see it in your eyes. It was the same as when you liked Tommy Fisher."

Amy's mouth fell open. "You said you would never talk about that again."

"So, I'm right?"

"*Nee*, not at all. You still haven't told me what happened at dinner."

"Sit down and I'll tell you." Once Amy sat down, Sarah said, "It was so embarrassing. My *mudder* started talking about the marriage as if it was definitely going to take place. I had to step in and say that Adam was merely visiting so we can meet each other. 'We're not getting married,' I said. 'Nobody's forcing us to do anything.' And then Adam didn't say anything. He just looked down. I don't think he likes girls who speak out too much. I think he likes quiet little mousey girls and I'm nothing like that."

"*Nee,* you certainly aren't," Amy agreed.

Her hazel eyes bulged. "What do you mean by that? Am I too loud?"

"*Nee*, you're just you. That's how you are. You're perfect."

Sarah giggled.

"Anyway, what do you think about him? Do you like him?" Amy asked.

"He's okay. I just have to get to know him better before I can have an opinion. It takes a while to understand someone and that's what my parents don't understand."

"Have you two arranged to go out or anything?"

Sarah shook her head. "He hasn't asked me out. My *mudder* suggested we go out just the two of us and he said that was a good idea, but then he never named a time. I was nearly going to suggest something, but then I thought it should be up to him, not me."

"I'm sure he will sooner or later."

"It doesn't matter, because I've got Elijah."

"When did you last speak with him?" Amy asked.

"We call each other at least three times a day. We have set times to call every evening, before and after dinner, and a time after breakfast. That way, neither of us is waiting around."

"That's good."

"I'm working up to asking Elijah to visit, but first I have to find someone he can stay with. It'll be hard for him to get away because he's needed on his parents' dairy farm."

"That would be difficult. Don't look at me. I can't have him here."

She laughed. "I know that, silly. As if that would be allowed."

"We know he can't stay with the bishop."

Both girls laughed.

"That would get complicated if he stayed there along with Adam. I'm dreading going to Lydia's wedding because that'll spur my parents on to me getting engaged to Adam."

Amy nodded. "I'm sure he's feeling the pressure too."

"I guess so." Sarah pushed her chair back from the table. "I should go and leave you to your work."

Amy glanced at the clock. "I've only got an hour and a half until Jonah gets home."

"*Denke* for lunch."

"You're welcome." Amy walked Sarah to the door, watching and waving as she drove away.

Amy did her best to put everything out of her mind and concentrate on her work.

CHAPTER 19

THE NEXT DAY, just as she was doing a difficult part of sewing the facing, Puppy scratched on the front door. Amy gritted her teeth and growled at the interruption. She left her sewing and clipped the leash onto Puppy's collar and took him outside. He sniffed around for about ten minutes before he finally chose a spot to do his business.

It was nearly time for Jonah to come home so she walked to the gate. And as she was hoping he would, Adam walked out of the bishop's house.

She turned to face him. "What do you do all day?" Then she remembered the bishop had lined up work for him.

"I sit around and wait for an opportunity to speak with you and Jonah."

She giggled at the unexpected answer. Not only was

it unexpected, it was inappropriate if he intended to marry Sarah.

He shifted his weight from one foot to the other. "By now you'll know all about me and why my parents strongly suggested I come here."

Amy slowly tilted her head to one side. *"Jah,* I do know that and a lot more about you."

"It's hard to be the only one who'll go against my parents and their choice of a spouse."

That told her he didn't intend to marry Sarah. "The first one out of your siblings?"

"Jah."

"Oh, is that the decision you've made? *Nee,* don't tell me. It's none of my business."

"I don't think it's any secret. Sarah told me when her parents left us alone that she already has someone she wanted to marry. I'm not going to stand in the way of true love or anything like that."

"Does that mean you'll be leaving soon?"

"Not too soon."

She nodded and looked down the road. As much as she liked him she didn't want to give him any encouragement until she was certain nothing would happen between him and Sarah. For now, she wasn't certain. Sarah said she preferred Elijah, but hadn't seemed to like it when she found out that Adam had spent time with her and Jonah. The only thing she could do was wait and see what happened.

THURSDAY AND FRIDAY were a blur for Amy, and she saw nothing of Adam. That was just as well because she spent almost those entire two days in a panic. She had Lionel come for the final fitting on Thursday and had been devastated to find she'd made an error with the length of his pants. They were an inch too short and she hadn't noticed that in his first fitting because she'd been concentrating on the jacket. Thankfully, she had enough length in the hem to let them out and redo them. It saddened her to realize she'd made such a simple and stupid error. It was Adam's fault. Her mind had been too focused on him and why he was there. After she found out his parents had pushed him there hoping he and Sarah would find love with each other, she'd been dreadfully worried.

Amy could not afford more errors like this. Her livelihood depended on her sewing and so far, her reputation was excellent. Once she'd altered the pants, no one would detect that there'd been an error. If all that last-minute sewing hadn't been enough, Lydia decided she wanted the waist of her dress taken in by one inch. It made the dress not as well fitted, and to make it right, she told Lydia she'd have to resew most of the dress, but there wasn't time. Lydia had insisted that's how she wanted it, but without doing the whole thing again. Amy ended up putting tucks in the waist area as a solution, given the time frame.

By Friday mid-afternoon, Lydia and Lionel had collected their clothing and Amy was able to breathe easy.

CHAPTER 20

THERE WAS ALWAYS a sense of satisfaction for Amy seeing a bride wear a dress that she had sewed. And today she sat in the second front row of Lydia's wedding in Lydia's parents' home. It was a special day and one that the bride and groom would remember and tell their children about. The dress looked lovely on Lydia and the alteration at the waist wasn't at all noticeable once the cape was over it. Anyway, any hasty sewing would've been outshone by the happiness on Lydia's face.

As usual, Jonah was sitting next to the bishop's son, Elroy, and Sarah was sitting with Amy.

When everyone was seated except the bride and groom, Lydia came down the stairs and joined Lionel and together they walked to the front of the room. They stood opposite the bishop as he gave a talk about the union of a man and woman being likened to Christ and His church. The husband looks after the wife just as Jesus looks after the church. Amy couldn't help noticing how good Lydia and Lionel looked together. He was tall and thin with dark hair and she was much smaller, with similar coloring. They looked a perfect match.

When the bishop had finished talking, a man Amy didn't know sang a hymn in German. Everyone stood and listened to his dulcet tones ringing through the house.

When a deacon stood to say a closing prayer, Amy's gaze fell to the floorboards and she tried to stop herself from counting the horizontal boards between the two rows of seats running down either side of the room. When she looked up, she wondered if she would ever have such a day as this for herself. Lydia would have this lovely day to remember for the rest of her life.

Amy wanted to be married one day, but apart from when she was at weddings, she'd given little thought to finding a husband. Her sewing and her brother took up all of her time. That was, until Adam had come to stay.

"It'll be you next," Sarah whispered to her.

Amy looked over at her and smiled and wondered who her friend was thinking she'd marry. "More likely you," she whispered back. She got an inkling that her friend was changing her mind when she noticed Sarah constantly looking slightly over her shoulder to her right. That was where Adam was sitting. She normally would have asked her friend outright if she was looking at Adam, but the truth might be too painful to hear especially on a day like today. How dreadful would it be if she and her friend liked the same man?

When they were heading out of the house, Amy was stopped by Thea Yoder, who asked Amy if she'd sew the wedding clothes for herself and her four attendants. After hearing she'd have three months to complete the task, Amy happily agreed and told her to stop by within the week to go over what was wanted.

Once the bride and groom were seated at the wedding table, Amy saw Lionel pass a gift to Lydia. He said something to her and she opened it and looked delighted.

Amy said to Sarah, "He's just given her a gift. How romantic."

"Good for some." Sarah slumped lower in her chair.

Amy looked at Sarah's sad face. "Don't be glum. You'll be next."

"I know." Sarah nodded.

The people at the wedding table were served their meals first, and everyone else served themselves buffet-style from the food tables.

Half an hour after the food was served, Amy noticed Lydia's mother, Lucinda, was in a fluster and Lydia was in tears.

"What's going on?" Sarah asked Amy, when she

noticed it too. "You find out. I have to run to the bathroom."

Amy hurried over to hear what was said. "Can I help you with anything, Lydia?"

"*Jah,* my wedding gift is missing and someone said Jonah likes collecting shiny and bright things."

Amy gasped and her fingers flew to her mouth. "*Jah,* he does, but only rocks and things."

Lucinda snarled, "This was a clear glass clock. He could've thought it was a rock."

Amy shook her head. "He didn't take it."

"It's missing," Lucinda snapped back.

"Do you think he swallowed it?" Amy said sarcastically, and then she pointed to him as he sat next to Elroy, eating. "Look at him. He hasn't got it. He hasn't moved from there since he came out of the *haus.*"

"I'll ask him." Lucinda raced over to Jonah and Amy hurried behind her. "Did you take the clock, Jonah?"

"Stop it. I told you he didn't." Amy could feel everyone looking at them.

Lucinda leaned down and tried to look him in the eye but he didn't look at her. Amy was just about to tell her to leave him alone again when Lucinda touched Jonah's shoulder and he jumped out of his seat and backed away.

Amy moved to stand between them. "Leave him alone. I told you he doesn't have it."

In a blind rage, Lucinda raised her voice pointing at Jonah. Amy felt as though she would pass out and then

Jonah started flapping his hands and breathing hard. This was the first time he'd had an attack at a community gathering. Everyone there understood what he was like and generally left him alone.

The bishop hurried over. "What's the problem?"

Amy got in first before Lucinda had a chance. "Lionel's wedding gift to Lydia is missing and Lucinda thinks Jonah took it."

The bishop looked at Lucinda. "Jonah wouldn't have taken it."

Lionel's mother hurried over and joined in. "He collects things and Amy didn't deny it."

Amy put up her hands and raised her voice. "Everyone, please, move away from him."

The bishop ushered everyone away and Amy could tell from some filthy looks coming her way that people weren't happy with her and Jonah. Soon, his breathing slowed and he calmed down.

"It's all right, Jonah. Let's go home." They walked to the buggy and she could see Jonah was feeling awful by his flushed cheeks and the panicked look in his eyes. After an attack like this he'd be exhausted for days.

Adam ran after her. "Amy, where are you going?"

She stopped still and so did Jonah. "Didn't you see what just happened?"

"*Nee.* I heard some commotion and I saw you walking away."

"Jonah was accused of taking the wedding gift."

His eyebrows drew together. "What wedding gift?"

She shook her head. "Don't worry."

"*Nee*, wait. Who accused him?"

She shrugged her shoulders not wanting to name names. "A few people. They've known Jonah all his life. Jonah's never taken anything. I'm just disappointed right now."

"Don't go. Let's sort this out."

"I've got to get Jonah home. I'll deal with it another time."

Amy walked away quickly and Adam hurried to catch up. "I'll drive you."

"*Nee* it's okay. I've got our buggy here." Amy kept walking. No one else had bothered to come after her. Adam had been the only one.

ALL THE WAY HOME, neither of them spoke. She left the buggy where it was and made Jonah a warm mug of chamomile tea in an effort to calm him. When he was looking a little better, she left him and unhitched the buggy.

When she'd done that and cared for her horse, she headed back into the kitchen and Jonah looked up at her. "I didn't take anything." His hands were cupped around the mug of tea.

"I know you didn't, Jonah. Don't worry about it. You can lie down in bed when you finish that if you want."

After Jonah finished his tea, he went to bed and

MY BROTHER'S KEEPER (AMISH ROMANCE)

stayed there all day. He had brightened a little by dinnertime but didn't want to leave his bed, so she placed his dinner on a tray and he ate it propped up in bed. Amy had to pray hard so she wouldn't be resentful toward the people who'd been so cruel to her brother.

CHAPTER 21

THE NEXT MORNING was Sunday and Jonah still looked pale and shaken, suffering the effects of the day before. She told Jonah he could stay home if he wasn't feeling well, and he was happy to take her up on the offer. She knew he was still feeling dreadful over the incident, but neither of them said another word about it. Hopefully, the gift would be found and Jonah's name would be cleared, and then she'd expect apologies coming their way.

Elroy came to see where Jonah was since Jonah normally traveled with the bishop's family to Sunday meetings and he normally waited close by for the buggy to be hitched.

Amy was glad to stay home, too, because she couldn't face Jonah's accusers. Last night, she'd been half expecting someone to knock on her door with an apology, but no one showed.

With Jonah having a sleep-in, she made herself a cup of *kaffe* and sat on the porch with a warm shawl around her shoulders.

She could do no work, today being a Sunday, but her mind was on one of her projects, sewing *kapps* for a woman who sold Amish clothing online. That was what she did when she didn't have special orders. Making aprons, *kapps* and capes was extra income. It wasn't much, but everything added up to help her get by.

IT WAS around midday when Sarah came to the house. The bishop and his family, along with Adam, still weren't home from the meeting.

Once they were seated by the fire, Amy said, "Did you see what happened yesterday?"

"I didn't see much except that Lydia and her mother were upset. I wasn't feeling the best. I spent most of the wedding in the bathroom, I was feeling so ill. When I came out, you and Jonah had left already."

"I'm sorry, I didn't know."

"It's okay. I'm feeling better now but not well enough for the meeting today. *Mamm* told me what happened and how someone accused Jonah of taking Lydia's wedding gift from Lionel. That's unforgiveable."

"*Jah*, I thought so."

"That's dreadful. I know you have enough problems without putting up with something like that."

"He was extremely upset about it."

"Did he do the hand-flapping thing?"

Amy nodded. *"Jah.* And you know how it makes him feel exhausted after?"

"I know, I remember." Sarah shook her head. "I'm so sorry."

"Nothing can be done about it now. I just hope the clock shows up somewhere and everyone will know he didn't do it and someone will have the decency to apologize to him and to me."

"Anyway, apart from all that, Lydia looked lovely in the dress you sewed her." Sarah smiled sweetly.

"She did. She looked good and the suit looked well-tailored too if I do say so myself."

Both girls laughed. It felt good to relax with Sarah. A laugh was what she needed to chase away the burdens.

"Have you seen or heard anything from Adam?" Sarah asked.

"Nee, I haven't seen him since yesterday. I haven't seen anyone. Oh, not so. I have seen one person. Elroy came to ask if Jonah was coming to the meeting."

"I think I might marry him."

"Who? Adam?" Amy asked.

"Jah."

Amy spilled her tea in her saucer, and she leaned over and put the saucer and cup on the coffee table. "Why this sudden change of heart? What about Elijah?"

"This is what my parents want and our two families

know each other really well. I don't want to create waves."

Amy knew Sarah would've created waves and a whole lot more to get what she really wanted. "So, you like him?"

"It's pretty hard not to like him."

"Hmm, and does he know this?"

Sarah giggled. "Not yet, but I told my parents and then they'll tell his parents and then a date will be arranged."

"You're not going to talk to Adam at all? It only makes sense you do."

"I'll talk to him when I see him next."

Amy already knew that she had talked to Adam before, and told him that she liked somebody else. As far as he knew there was nothing between him and Sarah. "You changed your mind pretty quickly."

Sarah pulled a face. "It's a difficult situation. They are both nice men, I'm just going along with what my parents want and I figure if I do that I can't go wrong."

"I'm happy for you." *But I'm miserable for me.* "Will you have to move?"

"*Nee* because his *mudder* told mine, he'd be able to move. He can find work here. That's another benefit. Elijah was stuck with the dairy farm. I would've had to move there. He might be upset when I tell him, but he'll get over it."

"I hope so," Amy said.

"Will you sew my wedding dress?"

"I will, of course I will."

Amy leaned forward and picked up her teacup and held it over the saucer half full of spilled tea, and started sipping the hot liquid. Would she forever be sewing dresses for other women while life passed her by? Just when she'd seen a spark of hope, a window into a new life, it was all taken away.

When they heard a buggy, Sarah jumped up and looked out the window. "It's the bishop coming home. Adam has jumped out of the buggy and is heading this way. He must be worried about me because I wasn't at the meeting." Sarah hurried over to open the door.

Amy stood and walked over toward the door too.

"Oh, Sarah, is Amy home?" He looked over Sarah's shoulder. "There you are, Amy. I've been worried about you and Jonah. Can I come in?"

Sarah stepped aside. "Come in, Adam."

He walked through the doorway and stared at Amy.

"We're okay. Jonah's shaken by what happened yesterday."

"*Jah.* That's why I was worried. I recall that it took him some time to calm down when I took the bishop's buggy on that Thursday." He stepped closer to Amy. "And how about you?"

She rubbed her forehead. "I'm fine."

"I'm sorry I didn't come to see you yesterday, but I was with the bishop's family and by the time I got home, your lights were out and I didn't want to disturb you."

Amy was pleased he cared.

"I haven't been well," Sarah blurted out.

He glanced over at her. "I'm sorry to hear that, Sarah. It's nothing contagious, is it?"

Sarah's mouth turned down at the corners. "I'm not that ill. I've just been feeling off."

"Still, you managed to drive over here." He looked around. "Where's Puppy?"

"He's in bed with Jonah. It cheered him up."

"Ah, I was right then."

Sarah asked, "Right about what?"

"I told Amy that dogs were good for *kinner.*"

"My *kinner* are going to have so many animals to play with."

"That's right because they'll be around the dairy farm. There'll be lots of cows." Adam chuckled, and Amy noticed Sarah didn't look too pleased.

"I'm not married to him yet. I might be able to be talked out of it."

Adam went quiet and the smile was wiped off his face. "Ah." He looked back at Amy. "Another reason I'm here is that the clock from the wedding was found."

"Where?"

"It seems a young girl took it. I forget her name. She was only three or four, and wasn't old enough to know what she was doing. Her mother found it in the family's buggy as they were getting ready to drive to the meeting this morning."

"I knew Jonah didn't do it," said Sarah.

Amy shook her head. "I had hoped everyone would've known that."

"You should get an apology from Lucinda."

"I'm not expecting one. I'm just glad the clock was found and everyone knows Jonah didn't do it."

Adam stepped back. "I didn't mean to interrupt you two. I just wanted you to know that, Amy."

"Denke for delivering the good news."

"I'm going home soon myself," Sarah said.

"I hope you get better soon, Sarah."

"I'm improving all the time. I'll just go home and sit in front of the fire. My folks would love it if you would stop by."

He smiled at her. "I would, but I agreed to go with Bishop Morgan and Fay. There's someone they want me to meet. He has some work that needs to be done on his house this coming week."

When he walked away from the house, Sarah whispered, "He's not here to help people out. He came here to get to know me, and that's all."

"From what I know of him, he likes to help people."

"Jah, and that's good, but I thought he'd be spending more time with me."

"And he might have if you hadn't told him about Elijah."

Sarah sighed. "I opened my big mouth too soon."

CHAPTER 22

THE NEXT DAY after Amy had seen Jonah off to school, Fay came running out of her house calling for her. Amy walked over. "What is it?"

"Tabitha called early in the morning asking for prayer for Sarah."

"What's wrong with her?"

"Stomach flu, she said."

"She was over here yesterday and she said she hadn't been feeling well, but I thought she was getting better."

"I'm just letting you know so you can add her to your prayers."

"*Jah*, I will. I should visit her. I can catch up on my work tonight after Jonah comes home from school."

"Okay, well, stay a distance away. You don't want to catch it."

. . .

Half an hour later, Amy was face-to-face with Sarah's mother, Tabitha. "I'm sorry, to hear Sarah's ill. It's nothing serious, is it?"

"*Nee*, I'm sure it's just the stomach flu."

"Can I see her or is she too sick?"

She shook her head. "She's sick. She's sleeping now. It's been coming and going the last few days."

"Could you tell her I stopped by?"

"Of course." And before anything further was said, Sarah's mother closed the front door. Amy was walking away when she heard, "Wait!"

She turned around and saw Tabitha again. "Sarah is awake and asking for you."

"Okay." As Amy walked into the house, she said, "I just hope you don't catch what she's got."

"I don't usually catch things."

"I'll give you a tonic before you go."

"*Denke*. A nice tasting one I hope." Amy grimaced.

"I can't guarantee it. I'll fix one now."

Amy headed up the stairs, and Tabitha called after her, "I'd say it was all the strange food she's eaten at Walnut Creek."

Amy walked into Sarah's bedroom to see her lying down sobbing. She flew to her side, kneeling on the rug next to the bed. "Shall I get your *mudder*?" She saw the empty cup of tea on the bedside. "Do you want me to get you more tea?"

She sat up holding her stomach. "I'm drowning in

146

herbal tea. That's *Mamm's* answer for everything—herbs and herbal tea. It's just not working."

"Can I get you anything?"

"Only if you can get me a new life." Sarah sobbed into her hands.

From the way Sarah was acting, Amy knew it was more serious than the stomach flu. Her first thought was that Elijah had called and said he didn't want to see her anymore. "What's going on? Is Elijah okay?"

Sarah looked between her fingers straight into Amy's eyes, and whispered, "I'm pretty sure I'm pregnant." She put her hands down and stared into Amy's eyes.

Amy's jaw dropped and she wondered if she'd heard correctly. "For real?"

Sarah looked away and nodded, and wiped a single tear from her cheek. *"Jah.* I'm certain."

After thinking about all the ramifications for her friend, she asked, "Does your *mudder* know?"

"Nee. She's practising all her herbal remedies on me and it just makes me feel worse. I can't even look at all that muck. I don't even believe in herbs." She breathed out heavily. "I truly don't know what I'm going to do."

"Elijah? Does he know?"

"I called him this morning and told him."

Amy gasped as the further realities sank in. "What did he say?

"He wants to marry me. I'll have to marry him now and I'll have to do it fast."

"I think that's the only way, and you did want to marry him anyway." She hoped she was making Sarah feel better, but she knew Sarah would get an extremely hard time from her parents about this. Everyone knew why couples got married quickly at a ceremony where no one was invited. A *boppli* less than nine months later always followed. It rarely happened, but it did happen.

"*Jah,* but then my folks will know that's why I can't marry Adam and then everybody in the community will know. We can't have a big wedding now like everyone else. It must be fast and probably just in the bishop's home. Not the bishop here, the bishop at Walnut Creek."

"I know what you mean." Amy nodded. "You could look on this as a happy thing. This makes up your mind between the two men and you told me you loved him when you got back here."

"I guess you're right. I have to forget Adam, and he seemed really nice."

"When will you tell your *mudder?*"

"I just can't." Sarah gave a nervous giggle and then shook her head.

Amy agreed, she couldn't think of anything worse to confess. It was shameful for everyone involved.

Sarah continued, "I just can't tell her, I just can't. I wonder if I should write a note. And then *Dat* will know and then that will be so embarrassing. Then all my sisters will find out and everybody will judge me. I'll have lectures about bringing shame upon the family and everyone telling me to repent. Everyone says not to judge anyone, but they'll all be judging me and wondering if I'm repentant, and Elijah too. It's none of their business."

"It won't matter too much because people will forget in time. We've had a few fast marriages over the years if you remember."

"I suppose you're right. In six months' time no one will remember." She stared at Amy. "Do you truly think so?"

"*Jah,* and if they don't forget, so what?"

Her mother pushed the door open. "People will forget about what in six months?" She eyed the two girls suspiciously as she stood there with her tray of health food biscuits and another large pot of herbal tea.

Amy held her breath, wondering if her friend would take this opportunity to tell her mother. *Not in front of me,* Amy screamed in her head.

"Nothing," Sarah said.

Tabitha put the tray on the nightstand. "What's going on? I can tell something's going on. Amy, what is it?"

Amy looked away and shrugged her shoulders, not daring to divulge her friend's secret.

Tabitha glared at Sarah. "Sarah, you're not pregnant, are you?"

CHAPTER 23

AMY FROZE and Sarah's eyes went wide and her mouth turned down at the corners as she sobbed uncontrollably. Tabitha sat down on the bed and put her arm around her. It was the exact opposite of what Amy was expecting. Screaming, maybe some yelling, or perhaps the cold silent treatment—anything but kindness.

Amy bounded to her feet. "I should go."

"You knew about this?" Tabitha yelled at Amy.

Amy gulped. She had guessed right about the yelling, but why scream at her? Amy opened her mouth but no words came out.

"I only just told her now, *Mamm*. Don't blame her."

"Who is the *vadder?*" she asked Sarah, now seeming far less understanding.

"Elijah."

She shook her head. "You both gave way to sins of

the flesh. This shouldn't happen outside of a marriage. You should both repent."

Amy felt sorry for Sarah because she looked so miserable.

"I'm repenting now," Sarah said in a small voice.

Her mother snapped back, "Only because of your morning sickness. I'm going to call his parents right now. Give me their number."

Sarah pointed to an address book on her nightstand. "It's the first number on the first page."

"Then I'm calling your *vadder*. He won't be happy." Tabitha rushed out of the room, almost knocking Amy out of the way.

Amy sat down on Sarah's bed. "The wheels are going to be set in motion now. Don't worry about anything. Your *mudder* has taken charge. Everything will work out. You'll get married to him and everything will be fine. And, I'm surprised she took it so well."

"What if he won't marry me?"

"Don't be silly, you just said he would. Besides, he loves you."

Sarah nodded. "You're right. He does love me. We love each other."

"This was probably all meant to be. You'll move to Walnut Creek and have a lovely life. You will write, won't you?"

"I will. I love Elijah and I love it in Walnut Creek. You'll have to visit me."

"It'll be hard with Jonah. I couldn't visit. You'll

come back though to see me and your parents, won't you?"

"I guess. That is, if *Mamm* ever talks to me again."

Amy leaned forward. "You might be in for a few rocky weeks until the marriage, but don't worry; after that, everything will be okay."

Sarah nodded. "I can see myself living happily with him and having many *kinner*. I guess it doesn't matter how we start out, but I won't get the large and happy wedding I always thought about."

"That's not really important. It only lasts for a few hours anyway."

Sarah pulled a face. "I'm not looking forward to everyone finding out."

"Not everyone will know, and besides you've gotten over the biggest hurdle and that was telling your *mudder*."

"*Denke*, Amy. I'm so glad you were here to give me strength."

Amy laughed. "I didn't really do anything."

"Will you stay here until *Mamm* gets back from calling everyone and telling them what a dreadful *dochder* she has?"

Amy reached out and placed a comforting hand on her arm. "She's not doing that."

When Sarah's mother came back from the barn, she seemed calmer. "Everything is arranged," she told Sarah.

"What do you mean?" Sarah asked.

"I've told Elijah's mother and I've called your *vadder* and he's delivering you to Walnut Creek tomorrow."

Amy grimaced inwardly. It sounded like they were packing her up like a package with a *do not return to sender* sign on her.

"I might not be well enough to travel. I've been sick the last few mornings."

"Sick or not you're going tomorrow. Just tell yourself you're going to be well tomorrow. I'll fix you a tonic."

Sarah pulled a face, and her mother turned to walk out, then stopped. She looked at Amy. "Amy, please don't breathe a word of this. No one needs to know."

"I won't tell a soul."

Tabitha nodded. "I believe you." Then she walked out of the room.

"Great!" Sarah's face soured. "Another tonic."

"Can I do anything for you?"

"Drink the tonic? Or at least toss it out the window for me?"

Amy giggled. "I wouldn't dare cross your *mudder*."

"I can't believe I'm supposed to leave tomorrow. I'm too sick to pack."

"I'll do it."

"*Nee, Mamm* can do it if she wants me to leave. She loves to organize people and things. Just say you'll write to me?"

"I will. And if you get a phone in your barn, give me

your phone number and I'll call you from time to time."

Sarah nodded, and then sniffed. "I'll come back here and visit you."

"*Jah,* please do that. I wish Jonah was able to travel, but he just can't."

Sarah sighed. "It looks like it's all going to happen. I no longer have a free choice."

Amy said, "You would've chosen Elijah anyway."

"Do you think so?"

"I've never seen you smiling so much. It was just like Lydia with Lionel. She wouldn't stop smiling either."

"Was I like that, too? But I doubted my feelings."

"*Jah,* it's probably just being away from him that's causing you to forget how nice he is. You were in love with him when you came back here. You told me so yourself."

Sarah nodded. "I think you're right and the *boppli* has helped me make the decision."

"That's right. You've got a head start on your family."

"Stop trying to put a positive spin on it. I know you're trying to be helpful, but …"

Amy looked at Sarah's stressed face. "Okay. I'm sorry."

"*Nee,* I'm sorry. I'm being awful and I can't stop myself. I'm just so embarrassed now. Everybody will know what Elijah and I have done."

"Don't feel too bad. Everyone makes mistakes."

"Mistakes? This is a lot more than that."

Amy tried to think of something else to make her feel better. "You're not the only one who's made that mistake in the world, so don't be so hard on yourself."

"You're a good friend, Amy. I hope you'll find happiness one day."

"I'm happy now."

"I know, but it's hard for you having Jonah all alone since your parents died."

"I love Jonah, and I'm doing my best." Sometimes it was hard, but she wasn't going to make things harder by dwelling on the bad times. "I'm blessed that I have an income from working at home so I can be there for him all the time."

"I'll be all right if you have to go. Just sit with me a few more minutes, and then I'll be okay."

After Amy sat with her for half an hour she walked downstairs to see Tabitha sitting on the couch sobbing. She sat down next to her. "Don't be too upset, Tabitha. Everything will be okay."

"My husband is furious and he's blaming me for not raising her properly."

"It's nobody's fault. Sarah is old enough to make her own decisions and she decided to do what she did. She's an adult."

"It's shameful."

"You might feel it's that way, but you'll soon have a grandchild."

"That's right, I will." A smile came to her face. "I will have a grandchild, but in Walnut Creek. I will hardly ever see the child."

"They might not always be there. You never know what the future will hold. And you can go visit them."

"Do you think they'll move here?"

"It's a possibility. People move all the time and if Elijah knows his *fraa* wants to move back here, then he might arrange his work so he can come here." She bit her lip remembering that Elijah worked on his family's dairy farm, so it wasn't likely that he could move. Especially when his siblings were all girls ... although some of them might find husbands who wanted to be farmers. Seeing that Tabitha had stopped crying, she continued, "And by then everybody would've forgotten what's happened. People don't remember things about others. People are mainly concerned about themselves and what's going on in their own lives. And besides, the Bible tells us not to judge others."

"It might *say* that, but it doesn't stop people from doing so. People judge all the time."

"You can't worry about it, Tabitha."

"*Denke* for your kind words, Amy. I really do appreciate it. You've been a good friend to my Sarah."

"She's been a good friend to me as well."

Tabitha cried some more. "I just don't know what's going to become of her."

Amy patted her on her back. "She's having a *boppli,* she'll be married to a man she's already proven she loves and they'll have a *gut* life together. Why don't you go up and spend some time with her? She leaves tomorrow."

"I will."

Amy left there exhausted. Now all her close friends were going to be married and who would she visit when she had free time? She doubted things would ever be the same after Sarah left.

CHAPTER 24

EARLY THE NEXT day after Jonah had left for school, Amy opened the door to Adam. He spoke before she had a chance to say hello. "Have you heard the news?"

Amy stepped out onto the porch. "About Sarah?"

"*Jah,* she left this morning to marry Elijah."

Everyone would know why the hasty marriage.

"I heard she was going and I visited her yesterday."

"Will you go on a buggy ride with me soon? I would say today, but I know you might have deadlines and such."

Sarah had been standing between them and it seemed they both knew it. Now she was gone, and Amy was looking forward to seeing what would happen between them. "I do have a lot of work."

"I'll help," he added.

Amy laughed. "You can't. Oh wait, there might be one way you can help."

"Name it."

"I'm sorry to do this, but can we stop by the fabric shop in town?"

He frowned at her. "You're making this a business trip?"

"I guess I am."

He chuckled. "If that's the only way I can persuade you to spend time with me, I'm fine with that."

ONCE ADAM HAD the buggy hitched and waiting at her door, she pulled on her coat and put on her black over-bonnet and then she stepped out into the cold morning air. When she stepped up into the buggy, Adam gave her a big smile. "Are you ready?"

She nodded. It seemed everything was going right for her for once.

"Are you warm enough?" he asked glancing over at her.

"I am."

"There's a blanket in the back."

"It's fine." They set off down the drive and for a fleeting moment she thought of Sarah and hoped she was okay traveling seeing she was feeling so ill. She hoped Tabitha's herbal remedy worked on her. She smiled as she remembered Sarah's reaction to her mother's tonics.

"How's Puppy?"

"Good. He's been a very good addition to our family. *Denke* once again for him. It was a lovely thought."

"As you pointed out before, I didn't *think*. I'm glad it worked out well anyway."

"It did. It was a good idea to give Jonah a pet to look after. I can see a difference in him since Puppy came into our lives."

He glanced over at her. "In what way?"

"He just seems more confident. I think that's what it is, and I'd have to say happier."

"That's good. Has he gotten over that whole business with the clock?"

"He has now. It took him a while. Anything like that takes him a couple of days to get over."

Adam shook his head. "You'd think that woman would've thought a bit more before she accused him."

"I've stopped wondering a long time ago why people do what they do. It's something we'll never know."

He laughed. "That's a very wise way to look at things."

"It's the way to look at things which causes the least amount of worry." Amy gave a little giggle.

"That's true."

"And what are your plans now that you won't be marrying Sarah?"

He glanced over at her again. "I'm not sure. I've got a few ideas, but I'll just have to wait and see how things develop."

She said nothing further, but she hoped he was talking about his relationship with her. It was quite possible he meant something else. The last thing she wanted to do was get her hopes up. Sometimes she thought he was interested in her. He was often at her place and constantly doing things for her, but until she heard it out of his own mouth, she wouldn't know for certain.

"What do you say we stop at the fabric store first and get that out of the way?" he asked.

"Good idea."

They trotted long in the buggy and she imagined they were husband and wife heading to town to do their monthly shopping. Even though they'd grown most of their own produce, there'd still be things they needed from the store. They would plan alone time, when Jonah was at school. They'd have mini dates where they'd go somewhere for a meal. A smile came to her face as she visualized what she wanted her future to look like.

He glanced over at her. "You're happy today."

"There's no reason not to be."

He said, "I thought you would be sad because you've just lost a friend to another community."

"I am sad for myself, but I'm happy for her. This is what she wants."

He looked at her, shocked. "It is?"

"It is."

"Is that what she said to you?"

She stared at him wondering why he was so intent

on asking something like that. *"Jah,* she did. You told me yourself that she told you she liked Elijah."

"I didn't know she was going to rush off and marry him." He shook his head.

"Did you expect to marry her?"

"Well, that's what my parents thought."

"You would've gone ahead with it if Sarah had wanted to?" She wished the conversation hadn't gone down this route, but she had to know. She didn't want to hear that he would've married one of her good friends if Sarah had agreed to marry him.

"We shouldn't talk about things like this."

"Possibly not, but now we've started and we should finish."

He took his eyes off the road and glanced over at her. "This is making you upset."

"Forget it." She shrugged her shoulders.

"It seems you might have gotten the wrong idea about things."

She made no comment and looked straight ahead.

"Anyway, let's not let what happened with Sarah ruin our day, okay?" He placed the reins in one hand and looked over at her.

She smiled and agreed. But how could she marry a man who would've married her best friend? What would've happened if Sarah hadn't found out she was pregnant? She might have kept the secret of what happened between her and Elijah and might have married Adam.

Amy looked at Adam, noticing how handsome he was. No wonder Sarah had been swayed when she met him again when she arrived back from Walnut Creek. Was Adam being nice to her because he felt sorry for her being the sole caregiver and provider for her younger brother and they were both orphans? Had she misread this entire situation?

When they walked into the fabric shop, he whispered, "I feel out of place."

She giggled. "I can't imagine why."

"What are you getting?"

"I'm looking for more of the same fabric that I made Lydia's wedding dress from. I just got another wedding job, Thea Yoder's, and she wants the attendants' dresses made out of that or something similar and she wants a slightly lighter shade. I'm going to get samples for her to view."

"Then shouldn't she have come with you?"

"That would've been good, but she works every day."

"Ah." He nodded.

"It won't take long."

She saw him look over the hundreds of rolls of fabric. "Somehow I don't think that'll be true."

He was right. It was an hour and a half later when they left there, and she had ten fabric swatches to show to Thea.

"I've worked up an appetite watching you make decisions back there."

"Me too." She wiped her brow with the back of her hand. "It was hard work."

"I saw that. Now, where's a nice place to eat?"

"They have a nice coffee shop next to the farmers markets where we'll be able to grab something."

"Okay. Can we sit down at a table and eat?"

"*Jah.*"

He raised his arm in the air. "Show me the way."

THEY HAD SANDWICHES AND COFFEE, and Amy enjoyed their time together. The time flew and Amy only got home half an hour before Jonah was due to arrive. Even though she hadn't gotten much sewing done that day, she realized from how relaxed she felt, she had needed the break.

AFTER AMY'S day with Adam, she had to push him out of her mind. She left everything in God's hands. She wanted to marry a man like him, but she knew she couldn't set her heart on him falling for her.

CHAPTER 25

MID-MORNING THE NEXT DAY, Amy was sewing when she got a surprise visitor. Lydia was back early from her vacation after her wedding. Since Amy had one less friend in the community now that Sarah had been sent away, Lydia was now her closest friend. She put her sewing aside, made a pot of tea, and together they sat in front of the fire drinking tea and nibbling cookies.

Lydia said, "I ran into Sarah in Walnut Creek."

"You were in Walnut Creek?"

"*Jah*, and she told me she's married to a man called Elijah."

"That's right. It was all very sudden."

"Did she tell you what happened?"

Amy nodded.

Lydia asked again, "Did she tell you the reason for her hasty marriage?" When Amy looked away, Lydia

167

said, "Hmm. I think we both know there's probably only one reason, isn't there?"

"Was she happy?" Amy asked.

"She was glowing. She said she's never been so happy. He's building her a *haus* on the side of his parents' land. They have a big dairy farm."

"That's *wunderbaar*. Things have turned out so well for her."

Lydia leaned forward. "She told me about Adam, and she thinks he would be a good match for you."

Amy rubbed her forehead. "We spent the day together yesterday. I can't work out whether he just wants to be friends or what's going on."

"If he's taken you on a buggy ride I think he'd want to be more than friends."

"I'm not so sure. Sometimes I think so and other times it's really hard to say. He had plenty of opportunity to tell me how he felt over lunch yesterday and he didn't. I mean, he even said something that made me think he would've married Sarah, if things had worked out differently."

"You mean if she hadn't run off."

"*Jah.*"

"He probably would've felt obliged to. Didn't his parents want it to happen, along with Sarah's parents?"

"I suppose so, but that was not something I wanted to hear."

Lydia shook her head. "You can't let things like that bother you."

"They do. It makes me feel not so special."

"You need to realize that things in life aren't perfect sometimes. We can't have everything exactly how we want. If he asked you to marry him, would you?"

"I honestly don't know. I've got Jonah to consider. He'd have to truly know what it's like having Jonah and always thinking if everything's right for him. What would Jonah think of having another person in the *haus*?" Amy sighed. "It would be nice. I wouldn't marry him if he would've married Sarah. I just want someone to love me and only me. Is there something wrong with that?"

Lydia chuckled. "Probably, because I think everybody can love more than one person."

"At a time?"

"*Jah*, of course."

"Hmm, that sounds a little odd. I just thought there was one person for everyone. Are you saying you could've married somebody other than Lionel?"

"*Nee.* I only would've married him."

"You were speaking in theory then and not going off your own experience."

Lydia shrugged. "Only trying to help. Don't listen to me. I don't know what I'm talking about. For me, it was only ever Lionel." She reached forward and took another cookie off the plate. After she took a bite and swallowed it, she said, "It would be good for you to have a husband. He would help you look after Jonah."

"Jonah is getting more capable of doing things for

himself. He constantly amazes me with what he's able to do and the concepts he's been able to grasp now."

"Is that right, or are you just saying that to make yourself feel better?" Lydia asked.

"*Nee.* It's true – he is getting so much better now that he's older."

"Ah, and about the wedding I feel so dreadful for my *mudder* saying that to you about Jonah. I hope you don't think I had anything to do with her reaction?" She stared at Amy.

Amy thought she'd been a little frosty toward her after that clock went missing. "I haven't given it any thought. Don't worry about it."

"I'm sorry. Anyway, who cares about a silly clock?"

"You got it back now?"

"I did. My *mudder* said she'll apologize to you next time she sees you, and she'll do the same with Jonah."

"It's not necessary."

"So, what can you do about your new man?"

Amy giggled. "He's not mine. The only thing I can do is wait and see what happens."

Lydia pouted. "Waiting is boring."

"That's the only thing I can do," she repeated. "I guess if he's not interested in me he'll be leaving soon."

Lydia leaned forward and patted her arm. "If he does leave that just means that he is not the right one for you."

"That's right."

"How's your sewing coming along?"

"I've got another wedding, but this time I've got plenty of time. I'm doing five suits, the wedding dress and the attendants dresses. They're coming for the fittings next week and until then I'll just keep doing my *kapps* and aprons. And I can get by. We can get by, I mean."

"That's good. I'm going to wait until I get the new *haus* in order and if I'm not pregnant by then I'll get a job somewhere. If I was as good as you at sewing, I'd do exactly the same as you."

"It's only a matter of practice."

"It helped that your *mudder* was so good too."

"*Jah*, she showed me everything. Sometimes when I'm sewing, I almost feel as though she's sitting beside me and encouraging me like she always did."

After Lydia left, Amy returned to her sewing. Then it was time to walk out and wait for Jonah. She half hoped that Adam would join her and Puppy at the gate, but he was nowhere to be seen.

The boys ran the last few yards toward her as they normally did, and patted Puppy.

Elroy stood, and asked, "Can we walk Puppy? We don't have chores today and Jonah said we could walk Puppy."

"*Jah*, but we thought we should ask you first," added Philip, the bishop's oldest son.

"That's fine. Are you going with them, Jonah?"

"*Jah*."

"Okay, stay away from the roads. Where will you walk him, Philip?"

"We'll stay within the property."

Amy nodded. "Okay, and remember, he's just a puppy. If you take him off the leash, he might not come back."

"We'll be careful," Philip said, and his brothers nodded in agreement.

Amy handed Philip the leash. "Since you're the oldest, you can be responsible."

"Denke," Philip said.

"You can come for milk and cookies after your walk."

"Okay. Come on," Philip said to the others as they walked past her.

Amy went back to her work, pleased with a few more moments to herself.

HALF AN HOUR LATER, Amy heard a dreadful commotion. She ran to the door and Philip and Jeff ran toward her. Philip called out, "Come quick, come quick! It's Puppy. He's gone!"

"What do you mean? He was on the leash?"

Jeff nodded while trying to catch his breath to speak and Philip cut across him saying, "He pulled away. The leash ripped right out of my hand and he ran up the road after a car. We ran after him. The car stopped and someone got out and grabbed him and then they drove away."

She gasped. "Someone stole him?"

"*Jah.*"

"They stopped and then someone got out and grabbed him," Jeff repeated.

"Where's Jonah?"

"He's sitting down by the road." Jeff waved his hand to indicate which direction.

Amy ran to find Jonah and the boys followed. She found him. His red cheeks were the only sign of his distress. Elroy was sitting next to him. She sat down on Jonah's other side.

"I want Puppy."

"What should we do? I'll tell *Dat.*" Philip and his brothers were distraught.

"First, describe this car. Did you get the plate number?"

"It was too … too … far," Jeff managed to say, puffing again.

"It was a white pickup truck," said Elroy.

She scratched her cheek wondering what to do. There had to be thousands of white pickup trucks around. "We can call the dog shelters and the pound, and we'll put up flyers all over the place. I'll go to the library tomorrow and get some printed."

"I'm telling *Dat.*"

As Philip ran to tell his father, Amy looked at Jonah. She wanted to promise him that the dog would be found but she couldn't. Careful not to touch him, she leaned a little closer and said, "We're going to do everything we can to get Puppy back, okay?"

Jonah didn't say anything. He probably knew the dog had gone forever.

Amy knew it was the worst thing that could've happened. She never should've allowed them to walk him and she told them to stay away from the road. There was no point saying anything about that now.

The dog was Jonah's best friend and constant companion and someone had taken him. Now he'd retreat further into his shell and he'd be how he was before Puppy came along.

A moment later, the bishop came out of the house with two sons on either side. "I'm so sorry this happened, Amy." He sat down on the ground beside Jonah and Elroy. "We'll do our best to find him, Jonah."

Jonah still didn't say anything.

"He's microchipped, and I have his paperwork." Amy stood up.

"That's a good start," the bishop said.

"We'll start trying to find him tomorrow. I don't think much can be done tonight."

The bishop stood up. "Let us know if we can do anything to help."

Amy nodded and wondered where Adam was. "I'll print some flyers from the library tomorrow and put them out everywhere. Maybe the boys can help distribute them."

"We will," said Philip.

"I'll get Jonah home. Come on, Jonah."

Jonah stood and together they walked back up the driveway. She could only imagine what was going on in his mind.

That afternoon, Jonah stayed on the porch as usual. As Amy prepared the evening meal, she prayed that the dog would find his way home, or that whoever took him found it in their hearts to bring him back. It was obvious he wasn't a stray and those people must've seen the children running after him. It saddened her that people could be so cruel.

CHAPTER 26

THE NEXT MORNING, she straightened Jonah's shirt as they waited for the bishop's children down by the gate. "I'll do everything I can to find Puppy today. I'm putting work aside and concentrating on this. I can't say I'll find him, but I'm sure going to try."

His expression didn't change. *"Denke."*

Then the other boys ran to meet him, and together they walked to school.

As Amy walked back to the house, she thought about Adam and how strange it was that he hadn't called in to see her last night about Puppy. Perhaps he'd travel with her to the library? Feeling brave, she walked over and knocked on the bishop's front door.

Fay opened it. "Has the dog been returned?"

"Nee. I'm going to the library to run off some flyers. I was hoping Adam would come with me and maybe we'll —"

"Adam's gone."

"What do you mean?"

"He's gone."

"Where?"

"I don't know."

"Didn't he say? Has he gone back home?"

"He left quickly this morning and that's all I know. He's an adult. I didn't think to ask him where he was going."

Amy breathed out heavily. She'd lost the dog and now she'd lost Adam. "I thought he might have told you in polite conversation where he was headed. I didn't see a taxi come to collect him."

"Morgan took him to town where he got a bus."

"Oh. That must've been when I was still asleep; I didn't hear a thing." Amy looked back at Fay. "Did he know Puppy was missing?"

"*Jah,* and he was very upset. He made some calls because he had the dog's details written down and then nothing came of it."

"Okay. *Denke,* Fay. I should go. I've got a big day ahead of me. I have to do what I can to get him back." She hurried back to her house upset that Adam hadn't even bothered to say goodbye to her or to Jonah. He hadn't even stopped by to say he was sorry about Puppy. Could he be angry with her for letting the boys walk him without her supervision? The dog had cost him a lot of money and now the dog was gone. That made sense. He was upset with her carelessness, and he couldn't see himself with a careless wife.

Amy drove her buggy into town and went to the library. That took the best part of the morning as she couldn't remember how to use the computer and had to wait to be helped by one of the staff. After she had a bundle of flyers, she handed them out to every business along one side of the street as she walked to the police station to make an official report.

"We don't usually handle this kind of thing," the officer at the desk told her.

"But the children saw the man take the dog."

The man shrugged his shoulders. "The best bet would be to try the animal shelters and that kind of thing. Wait a minute." He tapped on the keys of his computer for a couple of minutes, and then handed her a sheet of paper from the printer. "Here's a list of local shelters and their phone numbers."

"Ah, thank you so much. You've been very helpful."

"I try."

She smiled at him, thanked him again, and made her way back to her buggy while stopping in every store on the other side of the street and asking if they'd put the notices in their windows. In her heart, she felt she'd never see Puppy again. It would've been better for Jonah to never have had Puppy and then he wouldn't have missed him. As Amy climbed back into her buggy, she realized it was the same as with her and Adam. She would've been better off never having met him. She'd had a taste of what it would be like to have a caring man in her life.

When Amy got home and unhitched the buggy, she called every place on the list she'd been given by the officer. None of them had Puppy, but she left her address and phone number with each one.

WHAT FOLLOWED WERE some of the longest and loneliest days of Amy's life. She cried herself to sleep two nights in a row. At one point, she was even angry with God for allowing her to experience a glimpse of happiness and then letting it be taken away.

When the bride-to-be and her attendants came for a dress fitting, Amy put on a happy face as though nothing was wrong. She'd wanted to stop sewing for weddings, but she couldn't because they brought in too much income. If she had the choice, she wouldn't have anything to do with weddings anymore because they made her think of Adam.

CHAPTER 27

TWO DAYS LATER, a taxi pulled up at Amy's house in the late afternoon. Amy barely looked up from her sewing as she wasn't expecting anyone and thought it was someone for the bishop. Jonah was home from school and was eating his cookies and milk on the porch.

When Amy glanced up, she saw it was Adam and he had a puppy in his arms. She jumped to her feet, so pleased to see him, and then she stared hard at the dog. Had he gotten a substitute? Was he trying to fool Jonah? That would never work and could go horribly wrong. Jonah would know straightaway. He placed the dog down, and Jonah ran to the dog and the dog ran to Jonah.

"Puppy!" Jonah called out.

Amy flung open the door and ran to Adam, just as the taxi left. "You came back."

"I was gone longer than I wanted."

She resisted the urge to throw her arms around his neck, and looked at Puppy. "Where did you find him?"

He chuckled. "I can tell you one little boy who's very happy." Puppy was licking Jonah all over his face.

"Where have you been, Adam, and where did you find him?"

"I registered the bishop's phone number from in the barn with Puppy's microchip. I got a call early in the morning the day I left. It was by chance I even heard the phone. Anyway, the dog had been left with someone two-hundred miles from here. The people who picked him up must've changed their mind about keeping him."

"Why didn't you tell anyone where you were going?"

"I just couldn't. I couldn't get anyone's hopes up. I thought it best just to leave and not say where I was going and then if I didn't find the dog ..."

She didn't wait for him to finish. "You must've known it was Puppy because of the microchip."

"I didn't want anything to go wrong and I didn't want to tell anyone until I had the dog safely in my arms."

"I suppose that's best. Are you happy now, Jonah? You've got Puppy back."

"I'm happy," Jonah said, and then he giggled and Amy's heart melted.

"I thought you'd gone because you were upset with me for losing Puppy. He cost you so much and everything."

He smiled and shook his head. "He was taken. It was no one's fault."

She felt tears forming in her eyes.

"Hey, didn't you once tell me you never cry?"

"Maybe."

"Actually, I remember very distinctly. You said it."

"Well, I think that was in the past because I'm crying now."

He chuckled.

"Are you staying at the bishop's tonight?"

He shook his head. "I think I've inconvenienced them long enough. I'm staying at a bed and breakfast in town."

"And then where are you going?"

"That depends on you."

She stared into his eyes. "Me?"

He nodded.

"What do you mean?" she asked.

"It depends on whether you'll marry me."

Amy froze in shock. "What are you talking about?"

"I fell in love with you the very first time I saw you."

Those were the words she'd wanted to hear. Inside, she was bursting with joy. "But I was so cranky with you then."

"*Jah. Jah* you were. And I loved the way you stood up for Jonah when I'd been rude to him. You were like a fierce guardian angel."

"But ... but you said you would've married Sarah."

He shook his head. "You misunderstood me if you thought I said that. I never would've married someone just because my parents wanted me to. Not unless I also wanted that same person. They might've wanted me to marry her, but they haven't met you yet."

"What if they don't like me?"

He shook his head. "That's not even possible."

She giggled.

"Will you marry me?"

She couldn't believe her ears and all she could do was stare at him.

He cleared his throat and tipped his head. "Or should I be asking Jonah if there's room for one more in your family?" Adam smiled at her and then sat down on the ground next to Jonah and Puppy. "Jonah, what are your thoughts on the subject of me marrying your *schweschder*, and if I can persuade her, we can all be a happy family together?"

"Just like *Dat*." Jonah continued to stare ahead as the puppy licked his chin.

Amy knew he approved, and Adam knew him well enough now to know that too.

He continued talking to Jonah, and Amy was pleased to have that space to get used to the idea before he again sought her answer. "We'll be a married couple and someday, I might be a *vadder*. I can be like your big *bruder*."

"I don't have a *bruder*." Jonah giggled at the puppy licking him.

"But if you had one would you want him to be like me?"

"Would you want him to be like me?" Jonah said.

Amy had never heard him make a reply like that. There was no expression on his face but he was trying to be cheeky or funny.

"*Jah*. I would. I'd be pleased to have a *bruder* like you. Do I have your permission to marry Amy?"

"*Jah*." Jonah answered in his usual voice, showing no emotion.

Amy wouldn't have kept questioning Jonah, she had never done that, but he responded so well to Adam. Tears rolled down her cheeks and she turned away so no one would see her.

Adam jumped up and turned her around to face him. "There you have it. Do you have any reason why you can't marry me?" He held her arms lightly as she raised her hands to dry her tears.

She shook her head. "None at all that I can think of. Not now that Jonah agrees."

"So, it's, '*jah*?' You'll marry me?"

She nodded. "I will. I'll marry you."

He reached down and took hold of her hand and

held it tight. She had thought this day would never come. She'd often dreamed about being married to a wonderful man but she had never seen it as a real possibility.

Then she remembered when one of her friends had chided her about rarely going out anywhere, telling her the perfect man wouldn't knock on her door. But that was exactly what Adam had done. *Gott* had showed her He could perform wonders and make the impossible possible.

SARAH CAME BACK for Amy's wedding, which was hosted by the bishop and Fay. Sarah was seven months along but merely looked as though she was wearing a large dress. No one would've known she was soon expecting a child.

The wedding was a joyous event, and Amy was delighted Adam had been right about his parents liking her, and they were soon comfortable spending time with Jonah too.

After their wedding, because of Jonah's limitations, they couldn't travel to visit people like other normal young Amish couples, but they didn't mind. The three of them were now a complete and proper family. She hadn't felt she belonged anywhere after her parents died, but now she had somewhere she belonged and someone she belonged to. Jonah would surely have felt the same even though he didn't know how to say so.

Adam bought a small house for them, one that could easily be added onto over the years. For Jonah's sake, the three of them and Puppy slowly transitioned from the bishop's place to the new house. Adam paid for the plumbing to be fixed in Amy and Jonah's late-parents' house and they leased it for extra income. They both thought it best not to go back to the old place.

Adam sold his buggy-making business to one of his brothers and opened a new business working from the large barn on their property. Jonah seemed to enjoy spending his free time watching his 'big *bruder*' work, and he helped Adam keep his tools properly organized. When asked about his brother-in-law, Jonah always replied, "Just like *Dat*."

No longer did Amy have to work so hard. She still worked, but only because she enjoyed it. Her favorite sewing was for weddings.

Adam and Amy went on to have a house full of boys. None of them were autistic like Jonah, but Adam and Amy wouldn't have minded if one or more had been. Their boys loved Jonah as though he was their big brother. Amy was certain he loved them back.

Thank you for reading My Brother's Keeper.

www.SamanthaPriceAuthor.com

THE NEXT BOOK IN THE SERIES

Book 8 The Amish Marriage Pact

Kate blamed her disgraced siblings for Michael's sudden disinterest in their budding romance. After what they'd done, she couldn't blame him for not wanting to marry her, but did he have to fall in love with her best friend and leave their Amish community?

Disappointment over his double standards and broken promise filled her heart with bitterness.

When a handsome and suitable Amish man shows his interest in Kate, can she open her heart to love again? Or will her heart forever pine for the man she'd promised it to all those years ago?

AMISH MISFITS

ALL SAMANTHA PRICE'S SERIES

Amish Maids Trilogy
A 3 book Amish romance series of novels featuring 5 friends finding love.

Amish Love Blooms
A 6 book Amish romance series of novels about four sisters and their cousins.

Amish Misfits
A series of 7 stand-alone books about people who have never fitted in.

The Amish Bonnet Sisters
To date there are 28 books in this continuing family saga. My most popular and best-selling series.

Amish Women of Pleasant Valley

An 8 book Amish romance series with the same characters. This has been one of my most popular series.

Ettie Smith Amish Mysteries
An ongoing cozy mystery series with octogenarian sleuths. Popular with lovers of mysteries such as Miss Marple or Murder She Wrote.

Amish Secret Widows' Society
A ten novella mystery/romance series - a prequel to the Ettie Smith Amish Mysteries.

Expectant Amish Widows
A stand-alone Amish romance series of 19 books.

Seven Amish Bachelors
A 7 book Amish Romance series following the Fuller brothers' journey to finding love.

Amish Foster Girls
A 4 book Amish romance series with the same characters who have been fostered to an Amish family.

Amish Brides
An Amish historical romance. 5 book series with the same characters who have arrived in America to start their new life.

Amish Romance Secrets

The first series I ever wrote. 6 novellas following the same characters.

Amish Christmas Books
Each year I write an Amish Christmas stand-alone romance novel.

Amish Twin Hearts
A 4 book Amish Romance featuring twins and their friends.

Amish Wedding Season
The second series I wrote. It has the same characters throughout the 5 books.

Amish Baby Collection
Sweet Amish Romance series of 6 stand-alone novellas.

Gretel Koch Jewel Thief
A clean 5 book suspense/mystery series about a jewel thief who has agreed to consult with the FBI.

Made in the USA
Coppell, TX
20 July 2023

19390446R00115